## THE PRINCE AND THE PEKINGESE

"You have come!" the Prince exclaimed.

"Yes," said Angelina softly. "I have come."

The Prince paused for a moment looking at the beautiful young woman in a way that made her tremble.

"You are so lovely and yet . . ." There was a throb of pain in his voice that made Angelina long to comfort him.

"Whatever we feel for each other, "she whispered, "I realize your country must . . . come . . . first."

The Prince looked up sharply.

"*We* feel for each other?" he repeated. "Tell me . . . what you feel for me."

Angelina shyly lowered her eyes, but his tone was rough and insistent.

"Tell me," the Prince said again.

And suddenly, as if it came from the very depths of her being, Angelina's clear young voice miraculously cried out:

"I . . . love you. I love you. I love you!"

Bantam Books by Barbara Cartland
Ask your bookseller for the books you have missed

Barbara Cartland's Library of Love series

Barbara Cartland's Ancient Wisdom series

Other Books by Barbara Cartland

RECIPES FOR LOVERS

# Barbara Cartland
## The Prince and the Pekingese

BANTAM BOOKS · TORONTO · LONDON · NEW YORK

THE PRINCE AND THE PEKINGESE
*A Bantam Book | March 1979*

ISBN 0–553–12638–5

*Published simultaneously in the United States and Canada*

*Bantam Books are published by Bantam Books, Inc. Its trade-*
*mark, consisting of the words "Bantam Books" and the por-*
*trayal of a bantam, is Registered in U.S. Patent and Trademark*
*Office and in other countries. Marca Registrada. Bantam*
*Books, Inc., 666 Fifth Avenue, New York, New York 10019.*

PRINTED IN THE UNITED STATES OF AMERICA

## To the Reader

The Author's Note is at the end of the book, but please do not read it until you have finished the story, as it will spoil the plot for you.

*Barbara Cartland*

# *Chapter One*
## *1902*

" *"The Queen, looking very beautiful, was wearing a grey gown, the bodice decorated with diamond star brooches graduated in size. These are among her favourite jewels..."* "

Angelina's voice died away as she realised that her grandmother, to whom she was reading, was almost asleep.

However, it would have been a mistake to leave the room until she was ordered to do so.

Accordingly, she put out her foot and pushed Twi-Twi, the white Pekingese that was lying at her feet, in a manner which made him snort indignantly.

Her grandmother awoke immediately.

"What is the matter with Twi-Twi?" she asked. "Does he want to go out?"

"I think so, Grandmama."

"Then take him! Take him at once!" Lady Medwin ordered. "You know he ought to have a run every four hours."

It was not quite two hours since Twi-Twi had been taken into the garden of Belgrave Square, but Angelina did not say so.

Instead she said:

"Very well, Grandmama, I will take Twi-Twi into the garden, and I hope you will be able to sleep."

1

"I doubt if I shall do that," Lady Medwin said with dignity.

Nevertheless, before Angelina had reached the bedroom door Lady Medwin's eyes were closed, and Angelina knew that her afternoon nap was likely to last for at least half-an-hour.

Free for a moment from the obligations which took up a great deal of her time, she ran up to her own bed-room on the second floor and put on a straw hat trimmed with flowers which matched her muslin gown.

It was very hot even for August, and ordinarily everybody would have left London for their country houses, or for a holiday at the seaside.

But the Coronation of King Edward VII, which was to take place on August 9, had brought the Imperial and foreign dignitaries back to England, and anyone who was of any importance in the Social World was to be present at the ceremony in Westminster Abbey.

The Coronation had originally been arranged for June 26, but early in the month the King had developed appendicitis.

Everybody knew that at first he had refused to contemplate postponing his Coronation, but on June 23 his Doctors told him that he had peritonitis, which would kill him unless he agreed to have an operation right away.

The newspapers had described in glowing terms how the new King, determined not to disappoint his subjects, had argued furiously with his Doctors.

Finally, to save his life, they had persuaded him to have the operation the next day.

The whole nation, and in fact the whole world, was shocked by the news and then overjoyed by the successful outcome of the operation.

Angelina, though she would take no part in such an important occasion, was well aware of the commotion it had caused.

Next door to her grandmother's house in Belgrave Square was the Ministry of Cephalonia, and she had been entranced by the excitement amongst the gold-braided and bemedalled officials who had all arrived at the Ministry in June, then had departed, and now had returned.

She made every excuse to take Twi-Twi for walks in the garden so that she could watch the excitements taking place outside the Ministry.

It was her own private little view of what the Coronation meant.

Although she had tried to persuade her grandmother to let her go with one of the servants to watch the procession from Buckingham Palace to Westminster Abbey, or even to stand outside the palace itself, Lady Medwin had refused to entertain such a suggestion.

"I will not have you gaping in the crowds like some milkmaid from the country," she had said firmly, "and anyway the servants are too old to stand for hours, which it would entail if they had to accompany you."

This was certainly true, for all the servants in the huge, rather gloomy house in Belgrave Square had been in her grandmother's service for many years, and were, as her father had said once, on one of his leaves from India, "on their last legs."

It was because they were so old that Angelina was allowed to go in the garden of Belgrave Square alone with Twi-Twi, without having a maid in attendance.

Hannah, who had looked after Lady Medwin for over fifty years, had rheumaticky knees and disliked having to go downstairs at any time except for her meals.

The housemaids, and there were three of them, came into the same category, and Ruston, the old Butler, could only with difficulty reach the front door after the door-bell had been rung half-a-dozen times.

To Angelina it was a relief that she could go alone.

It was a tremendous effort to get anyone to accompany her to the shops, and sometimes she thought that in the whole of London she knew only one small oasis, in the shape of Belgrave Square.

But for the moment she was quite content to spend as much time as possible in the garden.

Peeping through the bushes, she could watch the excitements taking place next door without anyone being aware that she was there.

Twi-Twi too was content to nose about amongst the shrubs, and it was in fact rather embarrassing to take him anywhere else.

This was because Pekingese dogs were still a strange breed, unknown to the majority of the British people.

Angelina had been extremely interested in the history of these dogs, which for centuries had never been allowed to leave China.

She had read about them everything she could find in books. Sometimes when they appeared in Dog Shows there were articles about them in the newspapers and magazines.

These she cut out and pasted into a scrapbook. Having learnt as much about them as was possible, she had told the story to so many people who were interested that now she knew it by heart.

It was as early as 565 A.D. that the Emperor Kao-Wei of the Northern Chow Dynasty gave the name Ch'in Hu, or Red Tiger, to a certain Persian dog.

He also gave it the rank and privileges of Chun Chun, which were closely allied to those of a Duke.

The dog was fed with the choicest meat and rice, and when the Emperor rode on horseback the dog rode on a mat placed in front of his saddle.

From this dog and from some others from the island of Melita, which were carried to China in the

Silk Caravans, was bred a little Lion-dog which became almost sacred.

They were given an Imperial rank, but the rest of the world knew nothing about them.

When the Rebellion took place, three English Officers, searching and burning the Summer Palace near Peking, found five little Lion-dogs guarding the body of a Lady of the Court who had committed suicide.

One was brought back to England by a young Captain named John Hart Dunne, which he offered to Queen Victoria.

Angelina's voice would always change when she got to this point in the story, because she felt it was so moving that the young Officer should have wanted to give the Queen the dog he had brought all the way from China.

Lootie, for that was what the Pekingese was called, therefore became one of Queen Victoria's dogs.

This was the first of the Pekingese dogs which were found in the Summer Palace to appear in England.

Lord John Hay, in command of the frigate *Odin,* brought home two, although not until two years later.

He gave them to his sister, the Duchess of Wellington, who began to breed from them at Stratfield Saye.

Sir George Fitzroy also came back to England with two Pekingese, and he gave them to his cousin, the Duchess of Richmond.

Angelina's father, Major-General Sir George Medwin, had heard about the Chinese Lion-dogs when he was in the East, and two years ago, when he came home on leave, he brought as a present for his mother a small, pure white Pekingese, which he named Twi-Twi.

Lady Medwin had at first been astonished at seeing such a strange-looking creature, but then became completely and absolutely captivated.

5

Her attitude was echoed by the rest of the household who became quite maudlinly subservient to Twi-Twi.

They fell over themselves to serve him his minutely cut-up meat or chicken on the best china plates and went out of their way to caress him on every possible occasion.

Twi-Twi, as a matter of fact, did not care for their touching him, and treated them with a disdain that Angelina was quite certain was due to the fact that he was acutely conscious of his own importance.

A one-man or one-woman dog, he attached himself to Angelina and paid very little attention to anyone else, although he sometimes condescended to be handled by Lady Medwin.

Otherwise, he stalked about the house with the dignity of a Mandarin and the imperiousness of an Emperor.

Angelina was delighted that he liked her, and in fact, when occasionally he wished her to stroke him, he gave her a small, affectionate gesture by nuzzling against her hand.

But more often than not he sat apart, regarding everyone with a cool, impersonal eye, as if they were subjects with whom he should not become too familiar.

To Angelina he was an excuse for escaping from the house, which made life far more interesting and amusing than it would otherwise have been.

"Come along, Twi-Twi!" she said now, as the small dog followed her from her grandmother's room. "We are going walkies!"

He understood that very well and did not bother to follow her to the second floor, but waited at the top of the stairs, knowing exactly where they were going.

With her hat on her fair hair and a light in her blue eyes, Angelina came running down the stairs.

She looked very much like a small pink-and-white

angel, or perhaps, in a different way, rather like a Pekingese.

Like Twi-Twi, she was very beautiful, but it was a child-like beauty, which was, however, in complete contradiction to her mind.

Angelina was not only intelligent but well read.

This was because, being so much alone and having so few companions, she had read every book that came to hand and had developed her imagination far more than other girls of her age.

When her mother had been alive they had lived in the country and there had not been enough money for trips to London.

But Angelina had been completely content with her mother, with the horse she rode, and with the big garden which was always untidy and overgrown because they could not afford enough gardeners.

Her father had been abroad with his Regiment so much of the time that while she was still small, often when he returned she had found it hard to recognise him.

Shortly after his wife's death, Sir George had been sent to India, in command of the forces on the Northwest Frontier.

Although Angelina had begged and pleaded with him to take her with him, he had said:

"Women are a confounded nuisance when there is fighting to be done, and anyway I have no time to look after you."

This meant that she must live with her grandmother, and the last year since she had been grown up she had not had any interest in attending School and having lessons.

With the greatest difficulty she had prevailed upon Lady Medwin to let her continue with her music tuition from a very aged man who had once played in a famous Orchestra.

7

But otherwise there were only books and more books, in which she could read of other worlds that existed outside the narrow confines of her own.

Then, following the consternation over the death of Queen Victoria, had come the excitement of the new King's Coronation.

The Cephalonian Ministry had opened its doors in Belgrave Square only the previous year, and it had given Angelina a new interest that she had not had before.

Of course, she knew where Cephalonia was, having, although she had been told never to mention it, a little Greek blood in her veins.

Because it was a forbidden subject, Greece was naturally the one thing that interested her most.

A large part of her small dress-allowance went on a subscription to the London Library.

She searched their catalogues for the books she required and they sent them to her by post.

She had first read the mythology of the gods and goddesses who had lived on Mount Olympus. Then she had followed the miseries that the Greeks had suffered under the foot of the all-conquering Ottoman Empire.

Cephalonia was a large island off the West Coast of Greece, and although Angelina could find little that was written about it, when she had first been told the name of the Ministry which was established next door to her grandmother's house, she had felt that it was fate that it should come there.

Now, as she came down the stairs with Twi-Twi following her in a more dignified manner, she thought that perhaps she would be fortunate enough to catch a glimpse of Prince Xenos.

She had seen him only once after his arrival in England, for the Coronation as it had first been planned.

Tall, dark, and handsome, she had told herself that he looked exactly as a Greek should look.

Then, before she had had little more than a quick glimpse of him, the whole party from Cephalonia had gone and there was only the elderly Minister left for Angelina to watch.

But now the Prince was back again, and he had in fact arrived the day before yesterday.

Angelina had been expecting him, and when she was not actually in the garden, peeping through the bushes, she had been able to look out through the drawn curtains of the large double Drawing-Room which occupied almost the whole of the first floor of her grandmother's house.

Ever since Lady Medwin had been confined to her bed in a room which overlooked the back of the house, the holland covers had been placed over the furniture in the Drawing-Room, the blinds had been drawn, and the heavy damask curtains had been pulled.

On the ground floor there was a Sitting-Room, which was known as the Study, for Angelina to use and it was actually far more cosy than the Drawing-Room.

But she thought what a waste it was to have a large, well-furnished room shrouded as if it were in mourning, and unlikely to be opened again, unless by some miracle her grandmother's health improved.

Lady Medwin was very ill and the Doctors who frequently visited her did not offer much hope that she would ever come downstairs again.

Angelina would tell herself dream-stories in which her grandmother suddenly got well and gave a party in the big Drawing-Room, inviting Prince Xenos of Cephalonia as one of her guests.

Angelina would picture the chandeliers glinting with light, and her grandmother arrayed in the tiara and diamonds which badly wanted cleaning and which she kept locked in a small safe.

She herself would have a white gown with three

ostrich-feathers in her hair, which she could have worn at Buckingham Palace if there had been anyone to present her.

Her mother had often described to her the beautiful pageantry that took place at Queen Victoria's Drawing-Rooms, which she had attended on innumerable occasions.

Because she was sure her own début would take place in the traditional manner, Angelina had looked forward to making her curtsey.

Now Angelina's mother was dead, her grandmother was ill, and her father away in India. There were no Balls, no parties, no presentation, and no sight of the Coronation.

Prince Xenos would be in Westminster Abbey and would drive in the procession to the Palace. He would see all the other Kings and Queens from Europe besides the King's innumerable relatives and of course His Majesty's special favourites.

Angelina read the newspapers avidly, for her own interest, and they were also the only way in which her grandmother could keep in touch with her old acquaintances.

Lady Medwin had to know how often the King's special friends were mentioned as being at Buckingham Palace, and the more gossipy newspapers would describe their appearance and make comments that sometimes were definitely innuendoes.

Every newspaper had noted that Sarah Bernhardt, Lady Kimberley, Mrs. Arthur Paget, and the King's current favourite, Mrs. George Keppel, would all have special seats in the Abbey.

Lady Medwin, when she was well enough, usually had some caustic but informative anecdote to tell about each person that Angelina mentioned.

"What will the Prince think of the women he will meet at Buckingham Palace?" Angelina wondered.

She remembered that Greek girls were very beautiful so therefore it was likely that his standards of beauty would be very demanding.

As she reached the narrow, rather dark Hall, old Ruston, who seemed to be permanently on duty there, saw her and came from the shadows, holding the key to the garden in his hand.

"Going out, Miss Angelina?" he asked.

It was something he always said, although it was quite obvious what she was doing, and as Angelina took the key from him she smiled and answered:

"Yes. It is a lovely day, Ruston. Far too nice to be indoors."

"That's right, Miss Angelina. You enjoy yourself amongst the flowers," he said, having some difficulty in opening the front door with his rheumaticky hands.

She looks rather like a flower herself, he thought poetically, as she picked up Twi-Twi in her arms and ran across the empty road to where, a little way to the left, there was a gate.

A high iron fence prevented entry into the garden by anyone who was not entitled to do so.

Each householder had a key, but Angelina found that very few of them bothered to use it.

Usually she and Twi-Twi had the whole place to themselves and it was the same this afternoon.

It was quite a big garden, for the Square was a large one, and in the spring it was a riot of daffodils, crocuses, lilacs, and syringa, and it had a wildness which made Angelina yearn for the country.

At this time of year the centre of the garden was neatly laid out with crimson geraniums, their beds edged with blue and white lobelias.

There were, however, some wild roses growing amongst the shrubs, and the trees with their thick foliage offered plenty of shade from the hot sun.

Two gardeners were paid for by the householders to keep the garden well watered so that the lawns were bright green, and when the geraniums were over, there would be a good display of dahlias, which were just coming into bud.

Angelina locked the gate behind her, which was one of the most stringent rules to which the owners of the keys had always to adhere, and then she put Twi-Twi down on the ground.

First thing in the morning he would usually scamper about, excited to be free, but as this was his fourth visit to the garden today, he took his time, noting that nothing had been changed since he had been there earlier.

After pretending to walk a little way towards the geranium-beds in the centre of the garden, Angelina doubled back, and, moving amongst the thick shrubs which prevented the passersby from looking into the garden, managed to get a good view of the Ministry.

She had seen the Prince, accompanied by the Minister, leaving before luncheon in an open carriage.

There had been two men in uniform sitting opposite them, and Angelina had guessed them to be Aides-de-Camp.

She had thought that they were either going to luncheon at Buckingham Palace or with some of the many Royalties who were packed into every available house and hotel in London.

The papers had said there was not room for one more person to stay in the Capital, and Angelina had longed to offer the empty bed-rooms in her grandmother's house.

She had known that such a thing would be impossible, although it was delightful to dream of some minor Royalty who might become their guest.

The doors of the Ministry were open.

As Angelina looked through the leaves she guessed, by the number of footmen in attendance and the fact that the red carpet was waiting in a roll at the top of the steps, that she would not have long to wait.

The livery of the servants was very smart, green

with a large amount of gold braid for the senior servants, and gold buttons engraved with the Cephalonian crest for the less important.

Through the open door she could see the bottom half of a huge crystal chandelier and the turn of a marble staircase.

The Cephalonian Ministry was much larger than her grandmother's house. This was because two of the mansions in Belgrave Square had been converted into one and a double door had been built in the centre.

It looked very impressive, with the big flag hanging over the portico, the flag whose colours always made Angelina's heart leap a little because it was so romantic.

Sometimes she dreamt that she was sailing over the seas to Greece, and that she would see for herself the land of Apollo, which, she had learnt from her books, had a strange light that was different from the light in any other part of the world.

When she awoke, she always knew that it was very unlikely her dreams would ever come true.

Perhaps if her father relented and let her join him in India, as she longed to do, she would, as the ship carried her down the Mediterranean towards the Suez Canal, pass Greece and perhaps have a glimpse of the islands that clustered round the south of that immortal country.

There was still no sign of the Prince, and Angelina felt impatiently that if he did not come soon, she would have to go back to the house.

When her grandmother awoke she would ring her bell, and when Hannah had shuffled in, her first demand would be for another hot-water bottle, and her second would be for her granddaughter.

"Send Miss Angelina to me, Hannah," she would say. "There is still quite a lot in the newspapers which she has not read to me. But first give me my looking-glass. I want to see if my cap is on straight."

Lady Medwin had in her youth been an acknowledged beauty, and she was very particular that the elegant little lace caps trimmed with bows of blue ribbon, which she wore on her thinning hair, should be correctly adjusted.

Once, after the Vicar had called, she had caught sight of herself in the mirror and realised that all the time she had been talking to him, her cap had been on her head at a very jaunty angle.

She had been horrified, and after this she always insisted, at least a dozen times a day, on looking to see if her cap was straight.

"Where can he be?" Angelina asked herself.

She thought that perhaps the party had not been so formal as she had expected and the Prince had found some charming and attractive lady from whom he could not tear himself away.

Angelina had not listened to her grandmother's conversations over the past two years without realising that Society Ladies were very feminine and fascinating and that they attracted the attention not only of their husbands but of other gentlemen as well.

It was not only the King who had current favourites who were the envy of his contemporaries. There were, it appeared to Angelina, a number of affairs involving every lovely woman of whom she had ever heard.

Lady Medwin, of course, talked mostly of the beauties she had known when she herself had entertained interesting and famous people.

But they had now grown old, and there was a new generation of beauties who had followed Mrs. Langtry, Lady de Grey, and the regal Duchess of Sutherland.

Angelina found that her grandmother knew very little about the younger women who were mentioned in the newspapers and whose gowns were illustrated in *The Ladies Journal.*

She tried to imagine who had captured the Prince's attention, and she wondered what he would say to her and if in fact he spoke good English.

Somewhere she had read that the top Society in Greece spoke mostly French amongst themselves, but it seemed to her almost a betrayal of their nationality.

How could they not be proud, very proud, to be Greek? Just as she thought her father and all his friends assumed that by being English they had inherited the earth.

She could understand her father feeling like that because he was in India.

After all, the British had conquered India and the Queen had become Empress of India, and the Viceroy was, in importance, the equal of any King in Europe.

'Perhaps one day Papa will be made Viceroy,' Angelina thought; 'then he could not refuse to let me stay with him.'

But she knew that this was very unlikely. Peers of the Realm who were very rich became Viceroys, not soldiers, and she knew that if he was asked, her father would far sooner be with his Regiment, fighting on the Northwest Frontier.

"Men enjoy war," her mother had once said bitterly. "It is only their wives, left behind, who hate it."

"Why should men like war, Mama?" Angelina had asked.

"Because it is an adventure, a challenge, and I think that is what all men, if they are honest, want," her mother had said sadly. "They find it dull to sit at home and have nothing to occupy their time."

She had given a deep sigh.

"Women lose their husbands to war, to their Clubs, or to another woman."

15

She had then realised to whom she was speaking and added quickly:

"It is time for you to practise the piano, Angelina. You are not to waste your time talking to me."

Angelina had not forgotten what her mother had said, and she wondered if one of her father's reasons for not having her out in India was that he had found somebody to take her mother's place.

Nobody could do it completely, she thought, because her mother had been so sweet, so gentle, and so very loving.

Was that what a man wanted, or was it something different?

It was difficult for Angelina to answer questions about human feelings and relationships because she knew so few people.

She had had a Governess in the country, when her mother was alive, and when she had come to live with her grandmother she had completed her studies at a small, very select School for Young Gentlewomen, in Queen's Gate.

She had found, to her surprise, that she knew a great deal more than did most of the other girls of her own age.

She was certainly more curious than they were when it came to learning.

All they wanted to talk about was what would happen when they "came out": whether their parents would give a big Ball or a small Ball for them, which men would ask them to dance, and whether they would be taken to Ranelagh, Henley, and Hurlingham.

As her grandmother grew steadily weaker from what had at first seemed to be only a slight affliction, Angelina had seen her own hopes of "coming out" fade slowly and relentlessly into the distance.

Sometimes Lady Medwin would say:

"I must get well and arrange a party for you. I am really out of touch with the hostesses who have daughters of your age, but it will not be difficult to see that you are asked to the right Balls."

But lately the only time she talked about Balls was when they were reported in the newspapers and she recognised the names of some of the guests.

'If only Papa would come home on leave again,' Angelina thought to herself.

At the same time, she was sensible enough to know that there was little reason for him to make the long journey from India only to see her.

"If I were a boy, it would be quite different," she told herself.

That was the truth of the matter.

Her father had wanted a son and it had been a bitter disappointment that she was his only child.

She supposed that he thought he had done his duty in leaving her with his mother, who, had she been well, would have entertained for her in exactly the right manner.

Angelina gave an exasperated little sigh.

There was no sign of the Prince, and she was quite certain that the time had been passed quickly since she had entered the garden and that her grandmother would be asking for her.

'If I do not wait for him,' she thought to herself, 'he will arrive.'

She remembered her Nurse saying often enough:

"A watched pot never boils!"

That was what she was doing now, watching the kettle, while the Prince was doubtless philandering with some beautiful, seductive lady and could not force himself to return to the Ministry.

'I wonder what it is like inside,' Angelina thought to herself.

She was quite certain that it must be very impressive, but as she had never been inside an Embassy or a Ministry and had only read about them in books, she had no picture in her mind with which to compare it.

Her father had told her once about the magnificent buildings that had been erected for the English in India.

First, the huge Viceroy's Palace in Calcutta, which had been modelled on Kedleston Hall, the most important of Robert Adam's Palladian houses in the whole of England.

There was also a Palace-like mansion outside Bombay, but that was not the same as an Embassy, and she tried to remember what she had read about the inside of the British Embassy in Paris, which had once belonged to Princess Paulina Borghese.

There was still no sign of the Prince, and as Angelina turned from where she had been standing for so long, she found that Twi-Twi was lying down on the grass, just behind her apparently quite content to be inactive.

"Come along, you lazy boy!" Angelina said to him. "Run in the sunshine. It will do you good."

As if to show him how to do it, she ran across the lawn, seeming, because she was so small and light, hardly to touch the ground with her feet.

Only when she reached the shrubs on the other side of the gardens did she look back to find that Twi-Twi was not following her but merely sitting up, watching her, a little patch of white on a carpet of emerald green.

Angelina felt embarrassed at having run in such an unladylike manner, but she told herself that there was no-one to see her and it really did not matter what she did.

"I must remember to bring Twi-Twi a ball," she told herself. "I am certain the servants over-feed him, and if I am not careful he will get fat."

She loved Twi-Twi when he was playful, but even then he still seemed to have a dignity which other dogs did not have.

She walked back slowly towards him.

"You are a lazy boy!" she said. "Now I am going to take you home, and when you are sitting sedately by Grandmama's bed, you will be sorry that you were not more adventurous."

Even as she spoke she heard the sound of horses' hoofs, and she swiftly returned to her look-out opposite the Ministry door.

This time she was rewarded.

Coming down the Square from the west she saw the fine pair of black horses pulling the open carriage in which the Prince had set out before luncheon.

The coachman on the box, with his cockaded top-hat and with the footman beside him, looked very impressive as he drove up to the front door with a flourish.

By craning her neck a little and standing on tip-toe, because she was so small, Angelina could see the occupants of the carriage very clearly.

The Minister was shorter than the Prince, who seemed, with his square shoulders and with his top-hat on the side of his dark head, to be even more handsome and more attractive than she remembered.

As soon as the footmen had rolled down the red carpet and opened the door of the carriage, one of the Aides-de-Camp stepped out first to stand at attention as the Prince alighted.

He said something, and although Angelina could not hear what it was, she saw the smile on his lips as he finished speaking.

Then he walked up the red carpet and in through the open door of the Ministry.

Her heart was beating quickly because it had been so exciting to see him.

Then, realising that the pageant was over and the horses were beginning to move away, she knew she must hurry home.

She picked up Twi-Twi in her arms, and, taking the key from her waist-band where she had inserted it for safety, she ran towards the gate and opened it.

As she did so, the carriage passed her and turned left at the corner of the Square, so as to enter the Mews at the back of the houses on that side.

Angelina locked the gate and, still carrying Twi-Twi, started to cross the road.

Only as she had nearly reached the opposite pavement did something happen that afterward she thought she might have anticipated.

The Ministry cat, a rather ugly ginger, came up from the basement to peer through the railings.

If there was one thing in the world Twi-Twi really disliked, it was the Ministry cat.

Angelina had always been convinced that the ginger cat was aware of the loathing in which it was held and that it deliberately taunted Twi-Twi with "words" which only he could understand.

Strange sounds that made Twi-Twi bark furiously often came from the other side of the high wall that divided the courtyards at the back of the adjacent buildings.

Looking up and down the Square and not realising that its enemy was held in Angelina's arms, the ginger cat emerged from the railings and onto the pavement.

As it did so, Twi-Twi, with an unexpected show of strength, leapt from Angelina's arms onto the roadway.

Too late the ginger cat realised its danger, and, having no time to retreat in the direction from which it had come, it went off with the speed of a greyhound down the pavement, up the steps, and in through the front door of the Ministry.

If the ginger cat could move fast, so could Twi-Twi, when he wished to do so.

It seemed to Angelina that there was just a streak of orange followed by a shaft of white lightning as they swept past the footmen who were rolling up the red carpet and disappeared through the open door.

There was nothing Angelina could do but run after them, hoping optimistically that she could catch Twi-Twi but knowing that it was extremely unlikely.

Without realising what she was doing, she ran up the steps of the Ministry and in through the open door.

There were several men standing round, but her eyes were on the ground, looking for Twi-Twi.

She saw him at the far end of the very large Hall, where he had apparently cornered the ginger cat behind a huge china vase that contained an aspidistra.

Thinking that at any moment there might be a massacre, she rushed forward and called:

"Twi-Twi! Twi-Twi!"

There was a shriek from the ginger cat and a ferocious growl from Twi-Twi, and then the cat by some acrobatic feat leapt to the top of the china vase and from there to the staircase.

It slipped through the banisters and disappeared, while Twi-Twi, defeated, could only gaze after it, growling.

Angelina bent down and picked him up in her arms.

"How could you be so naughty?" she asked.

Then as she turned round she found herself confronted by the man she had just been watching—the Prince!

Without his tall hat, he was looking even more attractive, she thought, than he had in the carriage, and as she stood in front of him he seemed much taller than she had expected.

For a moment her eyes met his and it seemed as if it was impossible to find anything to say.

Then, conscious that there were other people in the Hall staring at her, Angelina murmured:

"I am ... sorry ... very sorry."

"Apparently your dog has an aversion to our cat," the Prince said.

As he spoke, Angelina realised that one of her questions about him had been answered.

He spoke perfect English, with just the faintest trace of an accent.

"I ... I am sorry," she said again, "but they are ... old enemies."

"Are you telling me that your dog and our cat are acquainted?" the Prince asked.

Too late Angelina realised that she ought to have curtseyed.

"I live next door ... Your Royal Highness," she said, with an effort to retrieve her bad manners.

"Then you have the advantage of me," the Prince said, "for you know who I am, but I do not know your name."

"It is Angelina Medwin, Sir."

"May I say that I am delighted to make your acquaintance, Miss Medwin," the Prince said, "and add that I am extremely curious about your dog."

As he spoke he looked at Twi-Twi, who was still trying to get a further glimpse of the ginger cat.

"He is a rare breed, Sir," Angelina explained. "He is a Pekingese."

"But of course!" the Prince exclaimed. "I should have known that. I have heard and read about these dogs in China, but I have never actually seen one before."

"Very few people have," Angelina said, "and the first one only came to England in 1860."

Even as she spoke, she thought it extraordinary that she should be giving what she thought of as "her lecture" on Pekingese to the one man she would have liked to listen to.

"That is what I read somewhere," the Prince said. "I believe they were acquired by the British when they burnt down the Summer Palace in Peking—is that right?"

"Yes, absolutely right," Angelina said, "but very few people, except yourself, Sir, have any idea where Pekingese dogs come from and why they look as they do."

"I feel certain that you know far more on the subject than I do."

The Prince was about to add something else but one of the Aides-de-Camp came to his side.

He spoke in Greek, and while Angelina had been making an effort to teach herself what was one of the more difficult foreign languages, she understood only one word: "waiting."

"Yes, of course," replied the Prince, nodding his head. Then to Angelina he said:

"I hope, Miss Medwin, that we may have the chance of meeting again, when we can talk of the fighting spirit of the belligerent Pekingese."

What he said seemed so amusing that Angelina gave a little laugh.

"I should be very honoured, Sir."

She knew that the Prince's eyes were twinkling and she felt that hers were too.

"What is this fierce dragon's name?" the Prince asked, showing by that one word that he knew quite a lot about Pekingese.

"Twi-Twi, Sir."

"Then I must thank Twi-Twi for introducing me to a very charming neighbour."

Angelina curtseyed a little lower than she would have done ordinarily, because she was apologising for her previous lapse.

The Prince bowed, and then an Aide-de-Camp appeared seemingly from nowhere to escort Angelina to the front door.

"Good-day Miss Medwin," he said, with a very pronounced accent.

"Good-day," she answered, and hurried down the steps without looking back.

As she walked home her heart was thumping in a very strange and peculiar manner.

"I have met him! I have met him!" she wanted to cry aloud. "I have met the Prince and he is even more wonderful than I expected him to be!"

# Chapter Two

Angelina carried Twi-Twi across the road, unlocked the gate, and went into the garden.

She was rather later than usual because the Doctor had called to see her grandmother.

After he had seen her, Sir William had shaken his head gravely but otherwise had not been very communicative.

As Angelina had accompanied him down the stairs, he had said:

"Give your grandmother everything she wants and make her happy. That is the best prescription I can suggest."

"I will do my best, Sir William," Angelina replied. "And thank you for coming to see her."

"I will call again next week, unless you send for me in the meantime."

He then looked down at her and smiled as if at the pretty picture she made.

"No need for me to ask you how you are."

"I am very well, thank you," Angelina replied, "but then I always am."

"You are young and you are lucky," Sir William remarked.

Then, raising his hat, he stepped into his closed brougham and was driven away.

As soon as he had gone, Angelina ran upstairs to her grandmother's room and said as she entered:

"Sir William seemed pleased with you, Grandmama."

Lady Medwin, who was wearing her most attractive lace cap and had daringly put a thin dusting of powder on her face, smiled.

"I like seeing Sir William," she said. "He has the courtesy which one expects of a Physician. Very unlike these modern Doctors with their rude manners."

She was referring to Sir William's partner, who had called on her last month when Sir William was out of London.

Lady Medwin had taken a violent dislike to him, had refused to do everything he suggested, and had made it clear that she did not wish to see him again.

Angelina, on the other hand, had found him rather intelligent, and she was sure that he was much more up-to-date in his methods than was Sir William.

But if he displeased her grandmother, there was certainly no point in him coming again.

Now, as she tidied her grandmother's lace-edged sheets, she asked:

"Is there anything I can do for you, Grandmama, before I take Twi-Twi into the garden?"

"No, thank you, dear child," Lady Medwin replied. "Take Twi-Twi for a walk, and when you come back you can read to me."

She gave a little sigh.

"It is such a lovely day. I would like to go out myself, but Sir William wants me to rest. In fact, he insisted that I try to sleep for at least two hours every afternoon."

"Oh, poor Grandmama! How tiresome for you!" Angelina exclaimed.

"I shall do what Sir William suggests," Lady Medwin said in a resigned voice. "And do you know, Angelina, he admired my cap!"

She paused before adding:

"Of course, it was slightly familiar of him and indeed not what I would have expected him to say, but at the same time it was rather flattering."

"You look very lovely, Grandmama," Angelina said sincerely, "and I am sure that any man who saw you would think the same."

Lady Medwin's old eyes seemed to light up for a moment, and it suddenly struck Angelina that, having been so admired and fêted when she was young, her grandmother must miss the compliments now that she was old.

"I tell you what, Grandmama," she said, impulsively, "I saw some pieces of lace in your drawer the other day and I am sure that some of it is very valuable. I will make you a cap so attractive and so becoming that Sir William will fall in love with you as soon as he sees you!"

"Really, Angelina, you do say the most outrageous things!" her grandmother protested.

At the same time, she was obviously pleased by the idea.

It took Angelina only a few seconds to put on her hat, but she lingered for a second to look at herself in the mirror.

Supposing she saw the Prince again?

If she did, would he think her attractive?

Then she remembered all the beautiful women he would be meeting at the parties being given for the Coronation, and she felt quite sure that she could not compete with them.

Inside the garden, Angelina put Twi-Twi down on the grass, then walked slowly and slightly self-consciously towards the shrubs where she could peep, as she had yesterday, at the front door of the Ministry.

Before she reached the shrubs she looked across the garden towards the beds of geraniums, and then felt her heart leap in a very strange way.

For the first time for ages there was someone else in the garden besides herself, and she saw that walking towards her now was the Prince!

She waited until he was within a few feet, feeling as if she were rooted to the ground, and then, remembering how badly she had behaved yesterday, she hastily made a deep curtsey.

"Good-morning, Miss Medwin!"

"Good-morning, Your Royal Highness."

"I was hoping that you would bring Twi-Twi for a walk in the garden. I understand you come here every morning."

"Several times a day, Sir."

Her heart was thumping in her breast and she found it hard to take her eyes from the Prince's. There was something in the way he looked at her which made her feel shy.

At the same time, she knew it gave her strange sensations she had never known before.

"I would like to talk to you, if you will allow me," the Prince said.

He felt that she hesitated, and he added with a smile:

"After all, we were introduced by Twi-Twi and Kruger, which I have discovered is the name of the ginger cat."

"Kruger!" Angelina exclaimed.

It was the name of the President of the Boers, against whom the British had been fighting up until May this very year.

The Prince smiled at her tone of voice.

"Not everyone, I understand, sympathised with England's aggressive war in South Africa."

"The Kaiser for one!" Angelina flashed. "But I did not think the Greeks ..."

"The Greeks are, let me say very quickly, pro-British," the Prince interrupted.

They smiled at each other as if their exchange of words had been somehow a little ridiculous.

Without consciously thinking of what he was doing, Angelina realised that the Prince was leading her towards a seat which was set in the shade of a large oak tree just in front of the largest flower-bed in the centre of the garden.

As they seated themselves, the Prince said:

"You are certainly very patriotic in this country— even when it comes to flowers!"

It had never before struck Angelina that red geraniums and blue and white lobelia were in fact the national colours, and she laughed as she said:

"It is, I am sad to say, in Belgrave Square our only decoration for the Coronation. Are they very impressive in the Mall and in Trafalgar Square?"

The Prince looked at her in surprise.

"You have not seen them?"

Angelina shook her head.

"My grandmother is ill and she will not let me go and stand in the crowds as I wish to do."

She felt that it sounded as if she was complaining, and she added quickly:

"I can understand that it would be impossible, but I am sure the streets are very pretty and decorative."

"Very," the Prince agreed, "and it is sad that you cannot see them."

"It was exciting anyway to see you arrive next door," Angelina said, "and I told myself that you would be my little bit of the Coronation."

The Prince gave a laugh.

"A very small bit," he said. "I assure you I have only just squeezed into the procession from the Abbey. There are so many more important Kings and Queens ahead of me."

"But you will be there, and it will be a very impressive ceremony," Angelina said in a dreamy voice.

As she spoke she was thinking of how magnificent the King would look and how regal when the Archbishop put the great jewelled crown on his head.

The Prince was watching her face.

"It will be just like any other Coronation," he said, "except that the British do these things so well."

"That is exactly what Mama used to say," Angelina replied excitedly, "when she told me about the Drawing-Rooms at Buckingham Palace."

"And you have not been to one yet?"

"No. My mother is dead, and my grandmother has been too ill to present me."

"I can see that your real name is Cinderella," he said with a smile, "and I wish I could wave a magic wand so that you could go to the Ball—or rather, in this case, the Coronation."

"Your Aides-de-Camp are very lucky that they can be in attendance," Angelina said, "but you could hardly arrive with a Lady-in-Waiting."

"I think everyone would be rather surprised if I did," the Prince answered.

They both laughed, as if the idea was amusing.

"Are you enjoying being in London?" Angelina asked when there was suddenly a little pause between them.

"Very much," the Prince answered. "I have been here before, but not for about five years. I have had so much to do at home."

"I have tried to find out about Cephalonia," Angelina said, "but there is very little about it in the history-books."

"For which we are exceedingly grateful," the Prince answered. "In some ways, we did not suffer as badly in the past as the mainland did. At the same time . . ."

There was an obvious pause.

"You are having trouble?" Angelina asked.

"A little," he replied.

She would have liked to ask him what it was, but

30

she felt that he might think it impertinent for her to be curious. So she waited, and after a moment he said:

"Tell me about yourself. What do you do when you are not taking Twi-Twi for a run in the garden?"

"Very little, I am afraid," Angelina replied. "I read the newspapers to my grandmother, practise the piano, and I do a lot of reading."

"So do I, when I have the time," the Prince said. "And what do you read?"

"A great deal about Greece."

"Of course," he answered. "It is obvious that you feel an affinity with the goddesses who are so much a part of everyone who loves beauty or who has Greek blood in them."

Angelina longed to tell him that she not only loved beauty but had a little Greek blood as well, but she thought that he might ask embarrassing questions, and anyway she had often enough been told never to speak of it.

"I am trying to decide which goddess you most resemble," the Prince said. "I think it must be the one who, to me, was the most beautiful of all—Persephone."

"I hope not!" Angelina exclaimed. "After all, she was incarcerated in Hades for six months at a time and was only allowed back when Zeus interceded for her."

Even as she spoke, she thought that perhaps in a way her present life was rather like being incarcerated in darkness.

Outside the house in Belgrave Square was a whole world of excitement, besides a Coronation and Kings and Princes to see and admire.

But for her there was only imprisonment in the quietness of a house filled with very old people.

"Exactly!" the Prince remarked.

She started and looked at him in surprise, because he had read her thoughts.

"Well, what can we do about it?" he asked, as if she

31

had agreed that he was right in what he was thinking.

"Nothing," Angelina replied. "But perhaps when Papa returns from India it will be different. If only he would take me back there with him!"

"Where is your father?" the Prince enquired. "I have learnt that he is an important General serving overseas."

Angelina was delighted that he had been interested enough to make enquiries about her, and she replied:

"Papa is on the Northwest Frontier, and he says it is not a place for women and therefore I cannot join him."

"I am sure your father is right," the Prince said. "I would hate to think of your life being in danger."

"It might be rather exciting," Angelina said provocatively.

"If you want excitement, there is plenty in London, I am quite sure of that!"

"Not for me! But you must not think I am complaining. Everything would be different if poor Grandmama were not ill."

"But she is, and therefore Cinderella cannot go to the Coronation."

"I can see one of the Princes who is attending it setting off in all his glory," Angelina said with a smile.

As she spoke, she suddenly realised that she was talking to the Prince just as if he were an ordinary person, without addressing him formally.

'I must remember to behave as I have been taught and as he would expect,' she silently chided herself.

The Prince, however, was obviously thinking of something rather deeply. Then he said:

"Suppose I invited you to drive with me this afternoon and see the decorations?"

Angelina looked at him in astonishment.

"No-no ... of course not ... I could not ... do that, Sir," she said hastily. "I have not told my grandmother that I have spoken to you and I am sure she would think it quite ... wrong."

She paused, then added:

"Even if I had a ... Chaperone."

"Quite frankly, I think a Chaperone would be a confounded nuisance," the Prince said, "but I want to show you the decorations—or, shall I say, I want to talk to you. I have a feeling that any moment you will disappear back into the bowels of the earth."

Two dimples appeared on either side of Angelina's mouth.

"Grandmama would not take that as a compliment."

"Stop teasing me and be sensible," the Prince said. "If I may not be allowed to take you to see the decorations, where else could we go?"

Angelina looked at him wide-eyed.

"I have a feeling, Sir, that whatever Grandmama might say, your Minister would not approve."

"My Minister does as he is told!" the Prince said. "And must we ask your grandmother's permission?"

Even as he spoke, Angelina remembered that Lady Medwin had just told her that Sir William had said she was to rest for two hours in the afternoon.

She knew that it was likely that he had prescribed for her grandmother a little medicine glass full of white liquid which always made her drowsy, even after she awoke.

Even if she was called after two hours of sleep, it was unlikely that she would want Angelina to read to her.

She thought to herself that the Prince was tempting her, but it was the most fascinating and exciting temptation she had ever had in her whole life.

"Say yes," the Prince pleaded. "We will not go anywhere where we might be recognised and talked about, if that is what you are afraid of. Perhaps we could drive in Hyde Park. I am sure Twi-Twi would enjoy the Serpentine."

Angelina did not reply that it was unlikely that anyone would talk about her, for the simple reason that she was unknown.

It suddenly seemed that to be alone with the Prince in Hyde Park, and sit by the Serpentine and talk to him, as she was doing now, would be far more exciting than seeing the decorations for the Cornation.

Her eyes were very large in her small face as she said:

"I know I ... ought to ... refuse Your Royal Highness's ... suggestion ..."

"But you will not do so," the Prince said in a triumphant tone. "If your father is brave enough to fight on the Northwest Frontier, then why should you not show a little courage in London?"

Angelina's small chin went up.

"It is not that I am afraid," she said. "It is just that I am not used to doing anything ... unconventional."

"Then it is about time you started," the Prince replied. "If we all did the right and conventional things, the world would be a very dull place."

He spoke gaily, but there was something in the tone of his voice that made Angelina think, although she had no grounds for doing so, that he too was showing courage, but in a manner which she could not understand.

"At what time will you be free?" he asked eagerly.

Somehow Angelina felt that he was hypnotising her into doing what he wanted.

One part of her mind wanted to go on protesting, while another part, far more straight-forward, told her that she was going to agree in the end, so why prevaricate?

"My grandmother will have her luncheon at about one o'clock," she said. "By quarter-to-two she will be ... asleep."

"Then from quarter-to-two I will be waiting on the other side of the Square," the Prince said. "I have dis-

34

covered that there are two gates to the garden, so you can let yourself in through the one on this side, and out through the one on the other."

"Did you . . . plan this before you came . . . here this . . . morning?" Angelina enquired.

The Prince did not answer for a moment, and because she was conscious that he was looking at her in a very searching manner, she dropped her eyes, and her long, curled-back eye-lashes were dark against the whiteness of her skin.

"When I saw you yesterday, I was determined to see you again," the Prince said in a low voice. "My Minister informed me that your grandmother had not called on him as the other residents in the Square had done, because, he understood, she was so ill."

"Grandmama has been bedridden for over a year."

"That is what I was told," the Prince said, "and I was wondering how on earth I could get to know you, until I learnt that you brought Twi-Twi every day into the garden."

He smiled as he said:

"If you had not come, I should have had to flourish Kruger in front of your house to lure him into the Ministry."

"Twi-Twi was obviously quite right in deciding from the very first moment he arrived that Kruger was an enemy," Angelina said.

"Which is something we could never be," the Prince replied.

She looked away from him towards the geraniums.

"I could never," she said passionately, "think of anyone who was Greek as an enemy."

"One day you must come to my country," the Prince said, "and I would like particularly to show you Cephalonia."

"I am sure it is very beautiful."

"Very beautiful," he answered. "It is, in fact, a small, mountainous Paradise."

Now Angelina's eyes were on his, and because he knew she was listening intently, he went on:

"From every peak of the mountains there can be seen the magical Ionian waves, and there are deep green valleys of arbutus, olive, orange, and lemon trees."

Angelina gave an ecstatic little sigh.

"Go on," she said. "I can almost see it. Tell me more!"

"The island has a sparkling girdle of deep-water caves, and high above is a bare indigo-and-umber plateau of volcanic rock, known as 'The Black Mountain.'"

Angelina did not speak, but she clasped her small hands together.

"It is crowned by the Venetian Castle of St. George, which was the Capital of the island until 1757."

"It sounds so beautiful! So very, very beautiful!" Angelina cried.

"It is a background for goddesses like yourself," the Prince said, "and the people of Cephalonia are as handsome as the country."

"I wish I could see . . . them."

There was silence, and she suddenly thought that perhaps the Prince would think she was asking for an invitation to the island, and the colour crept into her cheeks.

She rose to her feet.

"I must go back, Your Royal Highness. Grandmama will not expect me to be out for very long and will want me to read to her."

"You will come this afternoon?" the Prince asked.

"Do you . . . really want me to . . . do so?"

It was the question of a child who is unsure, uncertain, and perhaps a little afraid.

"I want it more than I have wanted anything for a very long time," the Prince said in a deep voice.

As if she felt she dare not listen to him, Angelina moved a few steps to pick up Twi-Twi.

He had been sitting on the grass near them, playing with a leaf that had fallen from a tree, just patting it gently with his feathery paws.

"I . . . I must . . . go."

Angelina's voice was soft and breathless.

"I will be waiting," the Prince said. "If you fail me, I myself shall come down into Hades and fetch you from the bowels of the earth back into the sunshine."

She flashed him a smile, then with Twi-Twi in her arms hurried across the green grass towards the gate.

The Prince watched her go.

Then with a sigh he picked up his top-hat, which he had put down on the ground beside the seat on which they had been sitting.

There was a serious expression in his dark eyes as he walked very slowly towards the Ministry.

* * *

Angelina read to her grandmother but afterwards she realised that not one word of what she had spoken had penetrated into her own mind.

All the time that she was reading about the preparations for the Coronation, which was to take place in two days, and the parties that were being given in every great house in London and every Embassy, she was asking herself how she dared do anything so outrageous as to drive alone with the Prince, even if it was only to the peace and quiet of the Serpentine.

She was well aware that it would be an unprecedented act on the part of any girl, especially one who had not been presented at Court and therefore could take no official part in Society.

It had been laid down very clearly that the first stage in the life of a débutante was to be acknowledged as a Social figure because she had been presented.

Until that had happened she could not enter the Royal Enclosure at Ascot, be entertained at any British Embassy anywhere in the world, or expect to be the guest of any of the acknowledged hostesses.

Angelina was certain that the Minister at the Cephalonian Ministry would not include her on his guestlist unless she could be vouched for as someone who had been accepted at Buckingham Palace.

But now, astonishingly, exactly like a fairy-story, she told herself, Prince Xenos had given her an invitation which she found impossible to refuse.

Inexperienced though she was, she was aware that it was not an invitation he would have dared to give to the Duchess of Devonshire's daughter or the Marchioness of Ripon's.

She had a feeling that she ought to consider it an insult. Then she asked herself what was the point of giving herself airs.

What would she gain by saying that she was too much of a lady to move anywhere without an attendant Chaperone?

And if she insisted on one, where would she find her?

She could hardly ask old Hannah to come with her in the Prince's carriage, or Emily, the housemaid, who was deaf and had very badly fitting false teeth.

Most of her grandmother's friends—and there were still a few who called to enquire after her—would, Angelina was sure, be scandalised at the idea of the Prince's invitation and horrified that she should consider accepting it.

But it would be an adventure, Angelina told herself, and when the Coronation was over he would go away and she would never see him again.

It would be something to remember—something precious that she could think about when she felt lonely, something which would be like the jewels that her grandmother kept locked away in the safe.

The only difference would be that the place where she would keep her memories would be in her heart.

Her grandmother had her luncheon taken upstairs on a tray, but, to save the servants trouble, Angelina had hers in the Dining-Room.

She often felt very small at the top of the big table covered with a spotless white linen cloth.

Round the walls stood a dozen heavily carved mahogany chairs, which were never moved because they never entertained and there was no-one to sit on them.

The Cook had been with Lady Medwin for as long as the rest of the servants—forty-eight years, Angelina thought it was.

Although she was an excellent "plain" Cook, she never troubled to try any new recipes, and adhered to the menu that Angelina's grandmother and grandfather had enjoyed when they were first married.

There was always a large joint of roast beef on Sunday, which usually meant that they had it cold on Monday and made into shepherd's-pie on Tuesday.

On Wednesday there would be leg-of-lamb. Two days finished that, and on Saturday there would be liver and bacon, which Angelina detested but which both Cook and Ruston declared was good for her.

"It makes red blood," they said, in a tone which made Angelina feel that she was either deficient or else her blood was slowly turning white.

The puddings too were always the same: caramel, bread-and-butter, "Spotted Dick," and cabinet-pudding, which, from the size that came into the Dining-Room, she gathered was appreciated in the Servants' Hall.

It was all very monotonous and she longed to have a party where, as Cook had informed her:

"The ladies and gentlemen always appreciated my *vol-au-vent* and the special way I have of cooking salmon."

Angelina could hardly expect a salmon all to herself, and though she longed for a little variety, she was too tactful to insist upon it.

Now into the monotony of her life had come the Prince, and she felt as if she were dreaming a very exciting dream and was terrified of having to wake up.

This could not really be happening, she thought, as she slipped upstairs after luncheon to change into what she thought was her prettiest gown.

To go with it she had a small but very attractive straw hat trimmed with blue ribbons that matched her eyes and a cluster of small moss-roses on the back of it.

Her grandmother was always very generous about her clothes.

Dressmakers came to Belgrave Square to show Lady Medwin their newest materials and sketches of how the gowns could be made up to suit Angelina.

The one she put on now was her best, and she hoped no-one would think it strange for her to be wearing, for no apparent reason on an ordinary day of the week, a gown she usually wore on Sundays.

Then she told herself that it was unlikely that Ruston's old eyes would notice that she looked any different, and she was certain that by the time she peeped into her grandmother's room she would be asleep.

She was right in that assumption, and she saw by her grandmother's bed an empty medicine glass, which told her, as she had expected, that Sir William had prescribed a sleeping-draught to ensure that her grandmother had a good rest.

She shut the door very quietly and tip-toed down the stairs, followed by Twi-Twi.

As usual, Ruston was waiting in the Hall.

"Are you going out, Miss Angelina?" he asked.

"Yes, Ruston," Angelina replied, "and as Her Ladyship is fast asleep, I shall stay in the garden while it is so nice and sunny."

"You do that, Miss Angelina," the old man replied. "It'll do you good to get the air."

He opened the front door, and Angelina, carrying Twi-Twi, sped across the road towards the gate.

She let herself into the garden, locked the gate behind her, and, without putting Twi-Twi down, hurried across the lawn to the opposite side of the Square.

Only as she unlocked the other gate did she wonder a little apprehensively if the Prince would really be waiting for her.

Supposing she had imagined the whole thing from beginning to end?

Sometimes Angelina's imaginings, or half-dreams, were so real that she would often ask herself if they were true.

This might be exactly that sort of dream—a fantasy of her mind, in which she had made herself and the Prince the leading characters.

As she stepped out on the other side of the Square, she looked apprehensively down the road.

The carriage was there!

As she appeared, the Prince got out of it and came towards her.

Hastily Angelina locked the gate, and by the time she had done so he was beside her.

"You have come!" he said. "You have really come!"

"You ... wanted me to?"

"I was afraid—desperately afraid—that you would not be brave enough at the very last moment."

She was about to protest, and he laughed gently.

"I am only teasing," he said. "I know you are as brave as that redoubtable Lion-dog you hold in your arms."

She dimpled at him but somehow she could not find anything to say.

They walked to the carriage and he helped her into it.

As he did so, he touched her arm and she felt as if a little shaft of lightning ran through her.

41

She sat down on the back seat and bent forward to put Twi-Twi on the seat opposite.

The Prince joined her, and as he shut the door of the carriage, she looked up in surprise to see that there was no footman on the box. Instead there was only the coachman.

The Prince explained without her having to ask the question:

"I thought the fewer people who knew what we were doing, the better," he said. "Alexis is a Greek and knew me when I was a little boy; he would never betray me, whatever I did!"

He smiled, then went on:

"He is also an incurable romantic, and when I told him I wanted to drive alone with a very lovely lady, he had the carriage ready and I sneaked out the back door without anyone being aware of it."

"Will there be a hue and cry when they find out you have gone?" Angelina asked.

"I left a note on my desk, addressed to one of my Aides-de-Camp, telling him I had a business appointment and not to worry if I did not return for several hours."

"You sound as if you were escaping from the Nursery, or from a rather severe School-Master."

"That is exactly what I am doing," the Prince said with a laugh. "They hedge me about and they cosset me. In fact, if you want the truth, they make my life a misery!"

He twisted round a little in his seat so that he could look at her.

"That is why," he went on, "if you are escaping this afternoon, so am I, and may I tell you, I find it a very exciting thing to do."

"It is very . . . exciting for me too," Angelina said.

"That," he replied, "is because we both know it is forbidden fruit."

42

"It is not as difficult for you, Sir, as it is for me," Angelina said.

"That is where you are wrong," the Prince answered. "There are a number of reasons why I should not be with you this afternoon, but none of them, may I add, are of the slightest importance beside the fact that I am with you."

The carriage had driven up Grosvenor Crescent and reached Hyde Park Corner.

As they passed through the gates Angelina exclaimed with excitement:

"Oh, they are decorated!"

There were flags and bunting and the Royal coat-of-arms surmounting the pillared gateway, and she looked at it almost rapturously while the Prince looked at her.

"I have an idea," he said. "I will tell you about it later."

"Tell me now," Angelina pleaded, but he shook his head.

"I have a feeling that if I do so, you will be thinking about it all the time we are together, and quite frankly, I would prefer you to think of me."

'It would be ... difficult to do anything ... else,' Angelina thought.

She knew, as they drove along towards the Serpentine, that she was vividly conscious of the man beside her.

It was not only that he was so handsome. There was, she thought, something very different about him from the other men she had met.

Not that she had met many since she had been grown up, but her father's friends had come to stay or called upon them when they had lived in the country.

Some of them had been young and dashing and said extremely complimentary things to her mother, who had laughingly protested that they were flattering her.

At the time, Angelina had hoped that the day would come when such elegant gentlemen would say flattering and perhaps flirtatious things to her.

But the way the Prince spoke was somehow quite different from the light-hearted, frivolous remarks that she had heard in the past.

Perhaps it was that his voice was very deep, or that he was speaking a little more formally in English instead of his own language, but there was a sincerity about him.

There was something else too—something magnetic—something which seemed to charge him with a life-force to which she felt that she responded in a manner that made her a little fearful.

It was as if he was taking possession of her, as if in some subtle, inexplicable way she was losing control of her own individuality and becoming a part of him.

Of course, such an idea was nonsense.

Angelina told herself that it was because she was so inexperienced and unsophisticated that the presence of the Prince should give her such peculiar ideas.

And yet they were there, and because she wanted to talk in a natural manner, she said:

"Do look at Twi-Twi, Sir! He is behaving as if the carriage were made especially to carry him wherever he wished to go."

"And why not?" the Prince asked. "After all, he is Royal, and in consequence he is entitled to all the privileges that should be accorded him."

"How do you know so much about him?" Angelina asked.

"I told you I had read about Pekingese, although actually I had never seen one," the Prince answered. "But last night at a dinner-party I asked the guests to tell me all they knew about Pekingese dogs, and I received quite a lot of extremely interesting information."

"How did they know so much?"

"Well, one of the guests was the Chinese Ambassador," the Prince replied, "and another was a gentleman who has studied the breeding of all dogs as a hobby."

"Oh, I wish I had been there!" Angelina exclaimed.

"I wish you had," the Prince answered. "At the same time, because you actually own a Pekingese I feel that you know more about them than all the books and all the authorities could tell me."

"I only know about Twi-Twi," Angelina corrected, "and he is a very special Pekingese to me."

"And of course you are very special to him," the Prince said, "so he is in fact the most fortunate Pekingese in the whole world."

Again Angelina's eye-lashes brushed her cheeks, but she was saved from a reply, for at that moment they arrived at the Serpentine.

The water reflected the blue of the sky, and when they stepped out of the carriage Twi-Twi ran ahead of them, his white tail held high.

They followed him to where there was a seat under the trees overhanging the water.

Angelina sat down and she thought that with the sunshine percolating through the leaves, the sound of the ducks in the distance, and the swans sweeping majestically past them, everything was enchanted.

She knew it was an enchantment that came from the man who sat beside her, his face turned to hers, his dark eyes looking, she felt, deep into her heart for something that was not apparent on the surface.

"This . . . is the Serpentine," she said in a dreamy little voice.

She spoke because she felt that the silence between them was somehow too intense and must be broken.

"And this," the Prince said, "is Xenos looking at Persephone and thinking she is the loveliest thing he has ever seen!"

Angelina looked away again.

"I do not ... think," she said hesitatingly, "that you ... should speak to me ... like that."

"Why not?" he asked. "The Ancient Greeks always spoke frankly to the gods. Sometimes they were quite abusive, and sometimes they merely spoke of their love and their admiration, and the gods accepted it as their right."

"I ... I am ... not Persephone."

"You are to me," the Prince replied, "but it is not you who must return to Hades after we have sat in the sunlight, but I!"

"Hades!" Angelina exclaimed in surprise. "You cannot be speaking of Cephalonia!"

"Not of my country, which I love," the Prince answered, "but of what I have to do for her. That will be Hades, as far as I am concerned."

"Why? I do not ... understand."

"Then I will tell you," the Prince said. "I did not mean to tell you, but somehow I have to do so."

He paused and Angelina glanced at him, then found it impossible to look away.

His expression was stern and she saw that the happy, laughing young man to whom she had talked this morning had gone and in his place was a man who looked older, and she knew that his feelings matched the darkness of his eyes.

"What is wrong?" she asked.

He looked away from her across the silver water and she felt that he was seeing something very different from what lay before his eyes.

"I have come to England not only for the Coronation," he said, "but for another reason as well."

"What is that?"

"I have come to arrange my marriage," he said, "with a Royal Princess."

He spoke abruptly, sharply, and Angelina sensed that there was pain behind the words.

There was a pause while she forced the appropriate answer to her lips:

"I ... I suppose it is ... expected that any ... Ruler should ... m-marry."

"It is something I swore I would never do unless I fell in love," the Prince said. "But because of the conditions that exist at the moment in my country, I have been forced into agreeing that I will take a wife who will please the people over whom I reign."

"Will it ... please them?"

"That is what I am told it will do."

He did not speak for a moment, then he said:

"Perhaps I should explain it to you from the very beginning: When my father was alive, part of the island over which he reigned demanded that we should amalgamate with the mainland, and that the Royal Family of Cephalonia should cease to have power."

"Surely that was ... wrong?" Angelina asked.

"The majority of the Cephalonians thought so," the Prince replied, "and when my father died and I came to the throne, it was thought that the opposition would die away because I would introduce reforms and all the things which my father had refused even to consider."

There was a faint smile on his lips as he added:

"My father was very conventional—very conservative. What had been good enough for his father was good enough for him!"

"But ... you were ... different," Angelina said softly.

"I have tried to be," the Prince replied. "I want to bring in new ideas, encourage innovations which I think are important to my people."

"And they appreciate them?"

"Some do," the Prince replied, "but some of the older folk deprecate any change. They say I am too impulsive, moving too quickly, the usual sort of thing."

Angelina felt that she could see it all so vividly.

"In the last two years things have got worse," the Prince said. "Someone—I am not quite certain who—is stirring up trouble. There are revolts, small in themselves but obviously important in a country as small as Cephalonia."

He sighed before he went on:

"I have to pay attention to my advisors. They tell me things are getting worse and a Royal marriage might divert the people's minds from talk of revolution and change the atmosphere."

"How could it do that?" Angelina asked.

The Prince smiled.

"The women like to feel that there is a woman to whom they can appeal, and women are, of course, half the population."

"So you are ... to be ... married," Angelina said, and wondered why her voice sounded as if it came from a very long way away.

"I have first to find a Princess who will accept me," the Prince said drily. "The Minister, and also my Prime Minister, who is with me, are quite confident that they will find one."

He brought his hand down rather heavily on his knee as he said:

"What could be more convenient than the opportunity of being in touch with such a large number of Kings, Queens, and Ruling Princes from all over Europe, because they are congregating in one place."

"Yes ... I can understand ... that."

"I should, at this moment," the Prince said, "be calling on the Crown Prince of some small Principality, who, I believe, has three unmarried daughters, each of them plainer and more *gauche* than the last!"

Angelina started.

The anger and contempt in the Prince's voice was very disturbing.

"Y-you should not ... speak like that," she said.

"Why?" he asked. "Why should I not be natural about it? Do you think I want to marry some woman who is interested only in my rank and not in the least in me?"

"I ... think she would become ... interested in you ... whoever she was," Angelina said. "But surely ... this is a very ... foolish way of getting married?"

"I have explained to you the circumstances."

"And I understand them," Angelina replied. "At the same time ... if you have a wife who does not love Cephalonia ... who does not understand what the Greeks have given to the world ... surely the result in your country will be to make it worse than it is at the moment?"

The Prince turned round on the seat to face her again.

"What are you saying to me?" he asked.

"I am saying ... I think I am saying," Angelina said, "that for a country to be happy ... it must be ruled by people who love it ... and perhaps who know ... love between themselves."

"Surely that is not to be found in any Court in Europe?" the Prince asked.

"That is not true," Angelina replied. "Perhaps when there is an arranged marriage they do not love each other at first, but if they are both attractive people, if they have the same interests, the same feeling for the country over which they reign, then they also find love."

She smiled and added:

"Remember how devoted Queen Victoria and Prince Albert were to each other."

"What you are really saying," the Prince said, "is that I am not seeking love. I am just resenting the fact that I have to marry someone I do not know."

"I am trying to say that," Angelina agreed, "and also something else."

"What is that?"

49

"The most important thing, as you have just said, is your country and the people who live in it. If there is friction ... if there is boredom and unhappiness in the Palace ... do you not think it will be known?"

The Prince did not answer, and Angelina added:

"A marriage in such circumstances might make everything far worse than it is already."

"You are right! Of course you are right!" the Prince exclaimed. "But how can I be sure that the woman I marry will understand what is required of her?"

"Because you must choose her yourself," Angelina answered. "You must see her, talk to her, and only when you are certain that she will learn to love Cephalonia will you allow your advisors to make representations to her father."

"Certainly what you are saying makes sense," the Prince said. "Why should you be so wise and sensible, when I have been so extremely obtuse about the whole thing?"

"Perhaps ... outsiders see more of the ... game than those who are participating in it," Angelina suggested.

"I certainly never expected anyone like yourself to advise me so sensibly."

The Prince's voice dropped as he went on:

"I have been pushed, badgered, cajoled, coaxed, threatened, and approached on this subject in every possible way, until I thought I should go mad!"

He put out his hand in an eloquent gesture as he said:

"Now, suddenly, a small goddess has completely changed my whole approach to the question."

"Is ... that true?" Angelina asked.

"But of course it is true!" he said. "I know now that it is exactly what I should do. There should be no question of making up my mind in the short time between now and when I leave London, which was my Prime Minister's idea."

He paused before he continued slowly:

"Instead, I will make a grand tour of Europe. I will find a Princess who understands what I am talking about. And, as you say, who understands the feelings, aspirations, and ambitions of the Greek people."

"That is what you must do," Angelina said positively. "I am sure then you will be ... happy."

As she spoke, she looked at the Prince and realised that there was a very different expression in his eyes from what she had expected.

"Happiness?" he asked in a strange voice. "Are you saying that that will bring me happiness? That, Persephone, is where you are wrong!"

# Chapter Three

Before Angelina could answer, a voice beside her
asked:

"Excuse me, but could you tell me what sort of
breed that peculiar-looking dog is?"

Angelina started, because they had been talking so
intently to each other that she felt as if she and the
Prince were alone in an enchanted world where no-
one could encroach.

Now she found herself looking at the curious eyes of
a middle-aged lady, encased in rustling taffeta, who
was looking not at her but at Twi-Twi.

He was watching a swan which had approached
rather near the edge of the water and was growling at
it in his throat.

"He is a Pekingese," Angelina replied.

"A Pekingese!" the lady exclaimed. "I do not believe
here is such a dog."

"He is Chinese."

"Chinese? Well, that accounts for it."

The lady spoke in a somewhat disdainful tone, as if
anything from China must be strange or slightly im-
moral.

Then, as if to assert herself, she said sharply:

"Personally, I am quite content with British dogs.
They are the best in the world!"

She turned and flounced away as she spoke.

Angelina looked at the Prince and they both laughed.

"I have always been told that the British are intolerably insular," he said.

"And very patriotic," Angelina answered. "Perhaps I had better buy Twi-Twi a red, white, and blue ribbon to wear round his tail."

The interruption had, for the moment, swept away the darkness from the Prince's face.

"I think I ought to go back," Angelina said. "If I am too long, the servants might go into the garden to look for me."

It was unlikely. At the same time, if her grandmother asked for her, it would be very difficult to explain why she had taken Twi-Twi anywhere other than the garden where she was allowed to go alone.

"I will take you back," the Prince said, "but I have to talk to you. There is so much I want to tell you, so much I want to ask you."

"There is . . . tomorrow," Angelina murmured.

"Tomorrow is the day before the Coronation," the Prince said, "and I have several engagements I shall be obliged to fulfil."

"Y-yes . . . of course."

At the same time, she felt her heart sink dismally.

Once the Coronation was over, the Prince would go away and she would never see him again.

There would be nothing to look forward to, no-one to peep at through the bushes and shrubs which faced the Ministry, and no-one to meet in the garden.

Even now she could hardly realise that she had been daring enough to drive with the Prince to the Serpentine and sit talking to him at the edge of the water.

It had been so exciting. No—that was not the right word—the one she had used before was better—"enchantment" was what described it.

As if he knew what she was thinking, the Prince said:

"I have to see you. You know that."

The way he spoke told Angelina, though she dared not put it into words, that this was an enchantment to him too.

"I have a suggestion to make," he went on.

"You said that once before, and perhaps you could tell me about it as we drive home. I really ... must go."

"I understand," he said.

Angelina rose from the seat to pick up Twi-Twi.

"You may be Chinese," she said, "but whatever any-one else may say, there is no other dog as beautiful as you in the whole Park."

"Are you assuaging Twi-Twi's feelings," the Prince asked, "or your own?"

"I was furious with that woman for criticising him," Angelina replied. "How could any dog be more beau-tiful?"

"One of your writers once said: 'Love me, love my dog!' and I think that applies to everybody. Their dogs are special to them, just as Twi-Twi is special to you."

"Of course," Angelina agreed. "And have you a dog of your own?"

"I have quite a number altogether," the Prince re-plied, "but only three in the Palace, which follow me everywhere. I would like you to see them."

Angelina wanted to answer that she would love to see not only the dogs but also the Palace where the Prince lived and Cephalonia itself.

But, carrying Twi-Twi, she merely moved beside the Prince across the grass to where the carriage was waiting for them.

As they went towards it, she glanced at the Prince from under her eye-lashes and thought that the stern look—or was it a grim one?—was back on his face and that once again he was thinking of the marriage he had to make.

She knew that it was something she herself would hate more than anything else—to have to marry a man with whom she had little or nothing in common, simply because they had both been born in a certain stratum of life.

'I am glad I am a commoner,' Angelina thought, with a little sigh.

At the same time, she was sure that the Prince need not worry as to whether or not his wife would love him.

How could anyone resist a man who was so handsome, so attractive, and so interesting in every way?

'Whoever she may be, she is very, very lucky,' Angelina thought to herself.

She wondered if the Prince's marriage would be reported in the newspapers. If it was, she would be able to read about it.

Then it struck her that if he married an English Princess and if they were married in England, there was no doubt that the wedding and every detail of it would be reported.

As usual, her imagination carried her away, and she was seeing a description of the bride's gown in *The Ladies Journal* and reading in *The Times* the list of distinguished guests present in the Church and at the Reception afterwards.

It struck her that now that she knew the Prince, he might invite her to his wedding, but even if he did, she would not be able to go if her grandmother was not well enough to accompany her.

She wondered if at his marriage he would look as he did now—stern, grim, and with an expression in his eyes that made her think he was hurt in a way that made her want to comfort him.

They reached the carriage in silence, the Prince

helped her in, and Angelina placed Twi-Twi on the opposite seat.

As the horse moved off, the Prince said:

"We now have very little time together. I want you to meet me tonight, and you must promise that you will do so."

"Tonight?" Angelina echoed in astonishment.

"Yes, tonight," the Prince said. "Listen, I have been thinking about it. It will be quite easy."

Angelina looked at him wide-eyed as he asked:

"At what time does your grandmother go to sleep?"

"She has dinner at seven-thirty and so do I," Angelina replied. "Then at eight o'clock I say good-night to her."

"What do you do then?"

"I sit downstairs and read. Or I go to bed and read there."

The Prince smiled.

"Then that makes it very easy."

"What do you mean?"

"I mean," he said, "that I will be waiting for you at quarter-past-eight, and if you cannot manage to be on time, then I will go on waiting."

"B-but I cannot..." Angelina exclaimed, "I cannot come! I cannot leave the house. Ruston, the Butler, locks the front door after dinner, and if I went out before he did so, I would be unable to get back in."

"Our two houses are built side-by-side," the Prince said. "Surely you can get into the Mews at the back, as I can?"

Angelina looked at him in astonishment.

She had never, all the time she had lived with her grandmother, gone into the Mews from the house.

If the carriage was wanted, one of the servants notified old Abbey, the coachman, and he brought the carriage round to the front door.

Then as she thought about it she realised that the door into the Mews was on the ground-floor level.

Once all the servants had retired to the basement for their supper, it was doubtful if anyone except Hannah and the housemaids, who slept on the top floor, would come downstairs again.

It was not their job to check if the door which opened into the courtyard was locked and bolted, and it was very unlikely that anyone except Abbey would be concerned with the second door, which opened from the courtyard into the Mews.

Like Ruston, Abbey was very old, and it suited him that the carriage was very seldom required and never in the evenings.

While Angelina was thinking, the Prince was watching her face.

"You see how easy it can be?" he asked. "I know, because it was the way I left the Ministry just now."

"But supposing . . . ?" Angelina began.

"Supposing someone finds out?" he finished. "But why should they? Even if they did, it could only be one of the servants, and surely they are fond enough of you not to sneak to your grandmother?"

Angelina laughed because it was so like School.

"I have a feeling they might do it for my own good."

"Then I will come and explain to your grandmother that it was all my fault," the Prince said.

Angelina gave a little cry.

"That would make it worse . . . much . . . much worse! Grandmama would be . . . horrified that we had not been formally introduced and that I have met you without telling her about it."

"Then we will just trust to our luck," the Prince said, "which has been exceedingly good so far."

That was true, Angelina thought.

What could be more lucky than that Twi-Twi should have been incensed by the ginger cat and taken her right into the Ministry so that she could meet the Prince?

"Perhaps it is not luck," he said in a low voice, "but that the gods have smiled on us. They can be very kind when they wish to be, and I am more grateful, than I can say that I found Persephone when I least expected to."

The deep note was back in his voice and it made Angelina feel very strange, almost as if there were little notes of music running up and down her spine.

"Will you come out to dinner with me tonight?" he asked.

Angelina did not speak and he went on:

"What we will do is to dine very quietly together somewhere where we can talk. Then, when it is dark, I will drive you round the decorated and illuminated streets so that you shall have your own special little bit of the Coronation with me."

Angelina felt her heart leap.

Could anything, she wondered, be more wonderful than to see the decorations, which she had longed to see, with the Prince beside her?

"I think this is ... one of my ... dreams," she said, "and I am ... afraid of ... waking up."

"I will not let you wake up," the Prince said, "not until we have been together tonight, and perhaps not for a long time after that."

Angelina thought that it could not be a very long time because he would be going away. But it would spoil the excitement that was rising in her, and which she felt was rising in the Prince too, if she said anything so practical.

Why not pretend that all this thrilling wonder would go on forever and that she would always feel as she did now, as if touched by a magic wand?

She was no longer Cinderella but she could go to the Coronation with Prince Charming—at least to a little bit of it.

"You will come."

59

The Prince made the words not a question but a statement, and because it was impossible to say no, because the idea of being with him was so irresistible, Angelina nodded her head.

"Thank you," the Prince said.

"I am really coming because I want to hear your story, and see if I can ... help you," Angelina said in a very low voice.

She knew, as she spoke, that she was salving her conscience, telling herself that apart from being selfish and enjoying herself as she had never done before, she was also helping someone who really needed her.

"I will tell you everything you want to know," the Prince promised. "Then you shall tell me how I can change the future, which until now has seemed exactly as I described it, like going down into Hades."

"I do not ... want you to feel like that," Angelina said. "Perhaps just by talking to me it will ... help you a little."

She made a gesture with her hands as she said:

"After all, I am very ignorant and know very little of the world. It is very presumptuous of me to think that in any way I can find a solution to your problems."

"You have already offered me one solution," the Prince said, "but it is not enough. I want a great deal more, Angelina."

His eyes met hers, and for a moment it was impossible for either of them to move.

Then, with a feeling of dismay, Angelina realised that the carriage had come to a standstill, and there were the familiar white-porticoed houses of Belgrave Square on one side and the green-painted railings of the garden on the other.

"We are ... home!" she said, a note of regret in her voice that she could not prevent.

"Yes, but only for a few hours," the Prince said. "And let me tell you, Angelina, those hours will seem very long to me."

The words were simple enough, but the way he said them made the colour come into Angelina's cheeks.

"I will ... come to the Mews ... if it is possible."

"It has to be possible!" the Prince said fiercely. "Make no mistake, Angelina, I have to see you. If you fail me tonight, I shall come knocking at your front door tomorrow morning!"

She looked at him to see if he was teasing or meant what he said.

To her surprise, she had the uncomfortable feeling that if she failed him, he would in fact come to the front of the house and demand to see her.

"I will come at ... quarter-past-eight," she said in a low voice as the Prince helped her and Twi-Twi onto the pavement.

As he touched her arm, she felt again that strange lightning-flash sweep through her, and because it was so disconcerting she found it hard to think.

Then, as neither of them moved, she said:

"If by any chance you have to do ... something else, perhaps you would tell your coachman to let ... me know if you ... cannot come."

"Do you think anything would stop me?" the Prince asked. "I swear to you, Angelina, if King Edward himself demanded my presence tonight, I would refuse him. I want to see you—I have to see you! It is going to be hard enough as it is to wait until eight-fifteen."

Again his voice disturbed her, and because she was shy, her eyes fell before his.

"I ... I will be ... there," she whispered.

Then, without looking at the Prince again, she ran towards the gate.

She opened it with her key and slipped into the garden without looking back.

Only as she hurried across the lawn towards the other gate did she remember that once again she had not curtseyed to the Prince and had forgotten, most

61

of the time that they were talking, to address him formally.

"It is no use," Angelina told herself, "we are past that."

Then she questioned her own thoughts.

Past what? And where were they going? The Prince was to be married. That was what he wished to discuss with her this evening.

Whatever else she might forget, she had to remember that he was a Royal Highness and as such had to find a Royal bride.

Angelina crossed the road on the other side of the garden and went up the steps of her grandmother's house, and she felt as she waited for old Ruston to open the door, that she was really Persephone.

It was as if she was leaving the sunshine behind as she stepped into the darkness of the Hall . . .

❊ ❊ ❊

For the rest of the day it was impossible for Angelina to think of anything but the evening ahead.

Half-a-dozen times she slipped up to her bed-room to open the wardrobe and decide which of her many gowns she would wear to have dinner with the Prince.

Her grandmother had started, at the end of last year, to buy her pretty gowns in which to make her début and be presented at court.

"I shall soon be perfectly well, dear child," Lady Medwin had said, "but perhaps it would be wise to ask if we could go to the last Court rather than the first."

It was only as the Season went by that Angelina realised it would not have mattered to which Court they were invited. Her grandmother would not be able to attend any sort of function which meant leaving her bed-room.

But the gowns had been bought, and because clothes amused Lady Medwin, she kept buying more.

"I shall be well enough to present you," her grandmother had said in January, and again in February, and, in a little weaker voice, in March.

The first "Drawing-Rooms" had taken place at the end of April and Angelina had read about them in the newspapers, and Lady Medwin had taken a great interest in the gowns worn by her contemporaries.

"Elsie would wear grey! Most unbecoming with her skin," she had remarked, "but then, she likes to think she resembles the new Queen. Such conceit! Alexandra of Denmark is a thousand times more beautiful than she could ever be!"

Lady Medwin had something rather caustic to say about all the other ladies presenting daughters.

"Green is an unflattering colour for Dora!" "The Duchess must have looked ridiculous in pale pink!" "Mutton dressed as lamb, I should call it!"

Angelina thought a little wistfully that she wished she had the opportunity of seeing the débutantes who had been presented.

She had a feeling that a great number of them were overshadowed by their mothers.

After all, being beautiful, sophisticated women-of-the-world, they could obviously outshine and outglitter any young woman emerging straight from the School-Room, with no experience of men.

And yet men, as Angelina knew from the talk at School, were all that the girls thought about.

She had heard them chattering away, hoping that young Lord "So-and-So" would not be married by the time they "came out," or that the Duke's son, who rode so recklessly, would not break his neck in the hunting-field.

Her grandmother told her that the social Mamas drummed it into their daughters' heads that they had to make a brilliant marriage.

There was no question of their entertaining romantic feelings for any nonentity or young man who had no money.

"And what happens if they fall in love, Grandmama?" Angelina asked.

"Then they just have to forget it," her grandmother answered. "At least until after they are safely married."

Angelina thought this over when she was alone.

She decided that her grandmother had meant that once they were married and had produced the essential heirs for their distinguished husbands, then they could have flirtations.

It was undoubtedly something which was indulged in by all the dashing gentlemen-about-town, who, like the King, had their favourites.

But she told herself that that was not what she wanted of her marriage!

She wanted to fall in love, just as in the fairy-stories, with someone who did not care who she was but loved her for herself.

'I am not rich and I am not important,' she thought 'so I cannot expect to have what is called a "brilliant marriage."'

However, she soon realised that her grandmother had very different ideas.

"You are very pretty, Angelina," she had said this year when once again she had been talking of taking her to a Drawing-Room, "but it is a pity that you are not taller. Tall women are the fashion at the moment. However, you will arouse a protective instinct in men, as the Duchess of Manchester did when she was young."

Lady Medwin laughed and went on:

"Louisa was actually as hard as nails, and so tough that no-one could ever get the better of her!"

"Did men find that attractive, Grandmama?" Angelina asked, wide-eyed.

"They never got beyond her eyes, my dear," Lady Medwin replied. "She caught the Marquis of Hartington, and he was faithful to her, or very nearly, for thirty years!"

Angelina had looked puzzled, but her grandmother had not explained, but continued:

"You move gracefully and you have a soft, melodious voice, which is very important. How I hate young women who speak in a strident manner!"

She paused to look Angelina over again, and added:

"Your greatest asset is that you look so very young, and when someone talks to you, you appear attentive."

"I am attentive!" Angelina said in surprise.

"There is nothing a man enjoys more," Lady Medwin said. "He likes to be the teacher, not the pupil."

Angelina had not really understood what her grandmother was talking about, but she was glad that she had some assets, even though when she compared herself with the descriptions of the great beauties who appeared in the newspapers and magazines, she thought she was sadly deficient.

Now, unexpectedly, unbelievably, Prince Xenos of Cephalonia wanted to talk to her and to take her out to dinner!

She was well aware that she was doing something so outrageous and so disreputable that if it was ever found out, her reputation would be ruined.

No nice girl would dine alone with a man! No nice girl would be seen in a Restaurant!

What was more, no nice man would ask her to do so.

But if she behaved as she ought to, Angelina told herself, what would be the point of sitting alone with a book when there was a handsome, attractive Prince wanting to talk to her?

"It may be wrong for me to go with him," Angelina told her Conscience, "but he really does need my help."

"And when you have given it—what then?" her Conscience enquired.

"I shall perhaps have made him a little happier."

"And what will you gain from that? He will marry his Royal Princess, and it will be cold comfort to think of them clasped in each other's arms, blissfully happy in the mountainous Paradise which you cannot enter."

Angelina faced her critical Conscience defiantly.

"I do not care!" she said. "It may be socially wrong, but it is morally right! Someone has appealed to me for help. It would not matter if it was a Prince or a pauper, a reigning Monarch or a crossing-sweeper. I am not a Pharisee who can 'pass by on the other side.'"

Her Conscience laughed rather rudely.

"Would you be so keen on giving your help if he was in fact an old, unattractive, rather dirty crossing-sweeper? Surely you are not pretending that the fact that he is a Prince has not a great deal to do with this sudden passion for being a Good Samaritan?"

"Yes, he is a Prince," Angelina said bravely; "but it is the Coronation, and I have been left out of everything this summer, even being presented."

It was a rather weak reply, she thought to herself. At the same time, it was true.

She never complained, never let her grandmother know how much she minded not going anywhere, not seeing anyone but her grandmother's old friends and the Doctors.

In her heart she had the inescapable feeling that time was running out. Soon she would no longer be a débutante. She would have missed everything that had seemed, when she was at School, to be the opening of the gates to a new world.

The girls had always talked as if their lives began at the moment they ceased doing any lessons and became young ladies rather than school-girls.

Angelina had been brought up in the same way, to

think that while she was a child, everything of any importance, anything that was entertaining or happened outside her home, must wait until she was officially "grown up."

Now that she *was* grown up, her life was more constricted than it had ever been in the past eighteen years.

She threw some last words of defiance at her Conscience.

"I am going with the Prince, whatever the consequences," she said, "and nothing and nobody is going to stop me!"

\* \* \*

The old housemaids had long given up helping Angelina to change in the evening from her day-gown into the one she would wear to dine alone downstairs in the Dining-Room.

It was as much as old Emily could do to tidy her room and turn down her bed, without having to come up before dinner to fasten her gown.

"I will manage, Emily," Angelina had said, because she felt sorry for the old housemaid.

Emily finally had taken her at her word, and, having tidied the room when Angelina had gone downstairs to the Dining-Room, she would not think of visiting it again until Angelina called her in the morning.

It meant that Angelina could put on one of her best evening-gowns without Emily being aware of it.

There was, of course, Ruston to worry about, but he was almost blind, and she knew that if she put a scarf round her shoulders he would not notice that her décolletage was lower than usual.

Also, instead of frilled sleeves on the gown she usually wore to dine alone, there was only puffed tulle over her bare arms, which made her look as if she were an angel encircled by a white cloud.

Nearly all her gowns were white, as became a débutante, but there was one she liked better than all the rest.

Of satin, which moulded her slim figure, it was trimmed with flounced tulle round the skirt and caught with little bunches of pale pink roses.

There was a bunch of roses at her breast and a little cluster of them which the dressmaker explained should be pinned in her hair.

Angelina had very little time to arrange these.

By the time she had said good-night to her grandmother, she had to collect her wrap, her evening handbag, her long white gloves, and Twi-Twi from her bedroom before she went downstairs to let herself out into the courtyard.

Angelina thought that her grandmother was the only person in the house who would not be surprised at her being elegantly dressed for dinner.

Lady Medwin herself had always worn elaborate and very beautiful gowns, and of course her jewellery, even when she had dined alone with her husband when he was alive, or with her family.

When Angelina's father had last come back on leave from India, he had remarked, as she came into the Drawing-Room before dinner:

"Really, Mama, you look as if you were going to a Court Ball. Sometimes when I am getting slack in the heat of India, I think of you and hurriedly change, even when I am dining alone."

"So I should hope, George!" Lady Medwin had said. "You must remember that an Englishman should always set an example to the lesser nations, especially those we have conquered."

"You are quite right, Mama," Sir George said meekly.

But Angelina noticed that his eyes were twinkling as he poured out the small glass of sherry which was all Lady Medwin allowed herself to drink before dinner.

Therefore, Angelina walked into her grandmother's bedroom, having taken off the tulle scarf that she had worn at dinner to deceive Ruston.

"How nice you look, dearest!" Lady Medwin said. "I am glad we bought that gown. It certainly suits you."

"I am glad you think so, Grandmama."

"I have decided that as soon as I am well enough," Lady Medwin went on, "I shall give a Ball for you. Tomorrow we will start making a list of all the people we wish to invite. Not only the young, of course. That makes a dance so boring."

"It will be lovely to have a Ball, Grandmama!" Angelina exclaimed.

She tried to sound as enthusiastic as she had the first time her grandmother had suggested such an idea.

But unfortunately with repetition the pretence had grown rather thin, especially as Angelina knew that such an effort would be quite impossible, as far as her grandmother was concerned, for a very long time.

"We will make out a list tomorrow," Lady Medwin said in a tired voice. "Good-night, dearest child. I feel I am going to sleep well tonight."

"I hope you will, Grandmama," Angelina replied. "Is there anything I can get you?"

"No, thank you, dear. Hannah has given me everything I want."

Angelina kissed her grandmother again and slipped away from the room.

Then she sped up the stairs to find that while she had been having dinner, Emily had prepared her bedroom as usual.

The greatest difficulty had been to eat as little as possible downstairs.

Not only was she looking forward to dining with the Prince, but Angelina was so excited that at the moment she felt that food would choke her.

For almost the first time, she found herself wishing

that Twi-Twi was not a fastidious, persnickety Pekingese, but a greedy spaniel who would gobble up everything she did not wish to eat herself.

But she knew of old that if Twi-Twi was presented with tit-bits, he would turn his nose up at them and walk away, leaving them lying conspicuously on the floor.

She had, however, a better plan. As soon as old Ruston had served one course, he would walk laboriously down the stairs to the basement to bring up the next.

This enabled Angelina to put back on the dish most of what she had taken on her plate.

It was easy with the soup, which she merely tipped back into the large silver tureen. It was rather more difficult with the fish, but she managed to make it look as if an extra slice had been cut from it by mistake.

But the apple-pie was the worst of all.

There were no more courses, since Angelina had decided that unless there was a party there was no need to add a savoury to the dinner.

As she took the smallest piece of pastry, she knew that at the moment it was the last thing she wished to eat.

"It would stick in my throat," Angelina decided.

She was therefore forced to cut it into small pieces and merely "mess about with it on her plate," as her Nanny would have said.

She hoped Ruston would not notice, but of course he did.

"You don't eat enough, Miss Angelina! You'd think that fresh air you gets would give you a healthy appetite."

"It has been hot today, Ruston," Angelina replied, "and I am never hungry when it is hot. Papa says the same, and that is why he has grown so thin since he has been in India."

She had been clever in starting Ruston off thinking about her father.

The old Butler adored "Master George," as he usually called him.

"Thin as a rake!" he said now. "I tells him when he was home: 'It'll cost you a fortune at your tailor, General,' I says, 'if you gets much thinner!'"

"You will have to speak to him when he comes on leave again," Angelina said, "and you know he always enjoys Mrs. Brooks' cooking."

"She's got all his favourite dishes planned for him already, Miss Angelina," Ruston said with a smile. "She never forgets what Master George fancies."

The old man was still reminiscing as Angelina left the Dining-Room.

One fortunate thing, she thought a little later, as she slipped down the stairs, was that there was no chance of Ruston creeping up on her silently.

He too had lost weight as he grew older, but he had never changed the size of his shoes. Now, as they were too big for him, he could be heard slip-slopping along the passages long before he came in sight.

The Hall was in darkness except for one gas-light, which Ruston would turn out last thing.

The front door was already bolted, and Angelina, with Twi-Twi in her arms, walked swiftly along the passage off which opened the Study and the Dining-Room.

Between these two rooms was the door which led out to the small paved garden.

On the wall that backed onto the Mews and faced the house there was some green trellis-work, up which climbed a rather anaemic-looking wistaria.

In the centre of the courtyard was a lead statue of a child holding a large dolphin in his arms.

It was meant to be the centre of a fountain, but a fountain would have caused too much trouble and therefore it was surrounded by ferns.

When these died they were replaced, but otherwise no-one paid much attention to their well-being.

The only people who could see into the small garden were those living in her grandmother's house and on the top floors of the houses on either side.

Angelina often peeped from her own window into the larger garden, also paved, which belonged to the Cephalonian Ministry next door.

Very occasionally she had seen grave-looking Statesmen or bespectacled clerks there, but otherwise there were only the gardeners who arranged flower-decorations for special occasions.

There had been a delightful show in June when the Coronation had originally been scheduled to take place, but the roses, the delphiniums, and the lilies had now been replaced with potted plants.

There were geraniums which made Angelina think of the ones the Prince had laughed about in the garden in the Square, and some brilliant-coloured begonias which were grouped round a statue which Angelina was quite certain was Grecian.

Unfortunately, it was partly obscured from her view by a tree which was planted on the Cephalonian side of the dividing wall but which extended over her grandmother's garden.

It made it impossible for her to see the adjoining garden as clearly as she would have wished.

She thought, from what she could see, that the statue was that of a goddess, perhaps Aphrodite, and she thought that she must remember to ask the Prince who it was and if it had actually been brought from Greece to Belgrave Square.

But there was no time at the moment to think about anything but getting herself safely from the house to the door at the end of the garden, which opened into the Mews.

"You must be very quiet," she whispered to Twi-Twi, "and not attract attention!"

There was really no possibility of her being seen or heard by anyone, and yet the fear was there.

All the servants would be downstairs having their
evening meal, but even so Angelina ran quickly over
the paving stones to open the door in the other wall.

As she stepped into the Mews, she felt as if she
were going into a new world.

The stables where the horses were housed and the
poky little windows of the rooms over them, where the
grooms lived, were all very different from the stately
dignity of Belgrave Square.

Then, before she had time to look round her, she saw
that only a few feet away from where she was standing was a closed carriage, and as she appeared the
Prince stepped out.

It was impossible then to see anything but the gladness on his face and the light in his eyes and not to be
aware that in his evening-clothes he looked even more
dashing and handsome than he did in the day-time.

There was a gardenia in his button-hole and he was
bare-headed because he had left his top-hat inside the
carriage.

He did not speak, but just took her hand and helped
her into the closed brougham and sat down beside her.

Then he pulled the door to, the horse started off,
and they drove down the Mews, the wheels rumbling
over the cobblestones.

"You have come!" the Prince exclaimed. "I convinced myself you would, and yet I was half-afraid
that something would stop you."

"I am here," Angelina said, "but I had to bring Twi-
Twi."

As she spoke, she put Twi-Twi on the seat opposite
her.

"Alexis will look after him while we have dinner,"
the Prince said.

"And perhaps," Angelina went on a little breathless-
ly, "you had better keep the key of the Mews door for
me. It is too big for my bag."

She handed it to the Prince as she spoke, remembering that it was easy to open the door from the inside, but it required a key to get back in.

It was something she might have forgotten had she not seen the key lying in a small dish inside the house when she opened the door into the garden.

It was kept there, she knew, for the convenience of the servants who might want to contact Abbey, who obviously had his own key.

The Prince took the key from her and slipped it into a pocket in the padding of the carriage.

"Do you want me to tell you how beautiful you look?" he asked. "I somehow did not imagine you with roses in your hair."

Angelina put up her hand a little self-consciously.

She had put them on so quickly after she had said good-night to her grandmother that now that she was half-afraid they were insecure.

"Do not touch them," the Prince begged. "Do not alter anything. You are just as I wanted you to be, only far more beautiful than I imagined!"

Angelina felt herself blushing and turned her face towards the window.

It was still light, but the sun had sunk in the west and the first evening stars had not yet appeared in the sky.

"Where are we ... going?" she asked in a voice that did not sound in the least like her own.

"I am taking you somewhere very quiet, not because I do not wish to show you off," the Prince answered, "but because I want to talk to you without being interrupted by music and too many people chattering round us."

"It will be ... very exciting for me ... wherever we go," Angelina said. "I have ... never dined in a ... Restaurant."

"I know you ought not to be dining in one now, especially with me," the Prince said. "That is why I think it was very brave and wonderful of you to do as I asked."

"Grandmama would be very . . . shocked!"

"So would a number of other people," the Prince answered, "and that is why I must take great care that no-one sees us or tries to make trouble."

"At the same time," Angelina said, following her own thoughts, "it is an adventure . . . a very big . . . adventure for . . . me!"

"For me also," the Prince said. "At the same time, I am afraid."

"Afraid?" Angelina questioned. "Why should you be afraid?"

"Because, if we are talking metaphorically, I am plunging deeper and deeper into a maze and I have no idea how to get myself out of it."

Angelina looked at him in surprise.

"I do not . . . think I . . . understand."

"I do not want you to," the Prince replied. "Not at the moment, at any rate. You are doing very strange things to me, Angelina, and I am not certain if they are pleasure or pain."

Again Angelina did not understand, and the Prince watched her face. Then he said:

"Stop me from talking like this. I want you to enjoy yourself tonight. I want your little bit of the Coronation to be something you will remember with happiness, very great happiness, for that is what I would wish you always to have, Angelina."

"I hope I shall," Angelina answered, "but I want you to be . . . happy too."

"That may be impossible," the Prince said, "but at least I have tonight, and that is very important to me."

"What are you doing . . . tomorrow night?" Angelina asked, because she felt a little embarrassed by the deepness of his voice.

"I have an engagement I cannot cancel," he

75

answered. "And the next night I must be present at the Banquet at Buckingham Palace—if it takes place!"

"If it takes place?" Angelina repeated. "What do you mean by that?"

"Remember what happened the last time."

"The King could not be ill again," Angelina said. "It would be too disappointing."

"There is no fear of that," the Prince said. "I saw him yesterday and he was in surprisingly good shape, after all he has been through."

"Then this time the Banquet will take place," Angelina said. "It would be terrible for all that food to go to waste a second time."

"Waste?" the Prince asked. "What happened?"

"It was not exactly wasted," Angelina answered, "but the newspapers reported that when the Coronation was cancelled, the officials at the Palace had no idea what they should do with the tons of food that had been ordered for the Banquet."

"So what did they do?" the Prince asked in an amused voice.

"There were two thousand five hundred quails, for one thing," Angelina said.

"Go on!" the Prince prompted.

"There were huge amounts of cooked chicken, partridge, sturgeon, and cutlets, not to mention all the fruit-and-cream puddings which would not keep."

It was something that had never struck the Prince amidst all the commotion of arriving in England and going away again.

"Tell me what happened!"

"They tried to think of a Charity which could be relied on to distribute the food fairly and discreetly," Angelina answered.

"And which did they choose?"

"The Sisters of the Poor."

She gave a little laugh as she added:

"It was the poor of Whitechapel, and not the Foreign Kings, Princes like yourself, and diplomats, who ate *Consommé de faisan aux quenelles, Côtellettes de bécassines à la Souvaroff,* and many other dishes created by the Royal Chef!"

The Prince threw back his head and laughed.

"I can quite see the predicament of having so much food and no-one to eat it. I must remember to tell my relatives about this when I go back to Cephalonia. They kept asking me details about the cancelled Coronation, but I had very little to tell."

"Well, now you will eat all those delicious dishes," Angelina said, "and see the actual ceremony in Westminster Abbey."

"Those things are amusing only when one has somebody with whom to laugh about them afterwards."

Angelina glanced at him quickly.

She thought that perhaps he was going to say that they could meet after the Coronation and he would tell her of everything that had amused him.

Instead, he stared ahead as if he was looking deeply into the shadows of the carriage.

Angelina realised that they were driving up Piccadilly, and there were decorations on the lamp-posts and on the houses they were passing.

She bent forward, and as she did so the Prince reached out to take her by the shoulders and turn her round to face him.

"No, I do not want you to look now!" he exclaimed. "It is more exciting by night, when everything is lit up. Then we will have the carriage open so that you can see it all properly."

Every nerve of Angelina's body was acutely conscious of the Prince's hands holding her shoulders and the fact that because he had turned her round, his face was very near to hers.

As if he too was aware that they were close to each

other and he was actually touching her, the Prince was very still.

In the quietness Angelina felt that he must hear her heart beating.

Then as abruptly as he had taken her, he released her, saying:

"We are nearly there. I hope you are as hungry as I am."

When they arrived in the Restaurant the Prince ordered a long and elaborate meal, but when it came, he and Angelina kept sending their plates away almost untouched.

Afterwards Angelina found that it was impossible to remember anything she had eaten.

The Restaurant, as the Prince had said, was very small, and it was in one of the streets leading off Piccadilly.

The moment they arrived, the Head Waiter led them down a long, narrow room to where at the end there was an alcove in which it was almost impossible to be seen.

The room was decorated in good taste and discreetly lighted and had a luxurious air about it which made Angelina certain that the dinner would be very expensive.

"This is a place for connoisseurs who enjoy good food," the Prince explained, "and also for people like ourselves who want to be quiet and not seen."

Angelina smiled at him as he concentrated first on ordering their meal and then on the wine-list.

When the wine came, Angelina thought it was like golden sunshine, but except when her father was home on leave she was accustomed to drinking very little, and she hoped it would not go to her head.

They talked of the Coronation, of Greece, of Twi-Twi, and of a number of quite ordinary things, until finally the plates were removed and there were only

the coffee-cups in front of them and the Prince's glass
of brandy.

He sat back in the comfortable arm-chair, which
was characteristic of the furnishings of the Restaurant,
and said quietly:

"Now we can talk about ourselves, and let me tell
you, Angelina, I have been able to think of nothing but
you the whole day."

"I have . . . thought about . . . you too."

She thought, as she spoke, that perhaps it sounded
rather forward to admit such a thing.

Then she told herself that she wanted to be honest
and straight-forward with the Prince, and not pretend to be coy as perhaps another woman might have
been.

The Prince took a sip of his brandy, then said:

"I told you this afternoon that I wanted to tell you
the whole story of myself. Do you really want to hear
it, or will it bore you?"

"Nothing you tell me would bore me," Angelina replied. "You also said I might be able to . . . help you,
and that is what I . . . desperately want to do."

"Why desperately?" the Prince asked.

Angelina dropped her eyes before his.

"I was . . . thinking this afternoon that I would want
to help . . . anyone who was in trouble," she said. "But
I particularly want to help you . . . because you are . . .
Greek."

"And also, I hope, because I am me?"

Angelina smiled.

"That is obvious. I do not know any other Princes."

"That is not what I meant," he said. "I would want
you to help me whether I was a Prince or a commoner."

Because he seemed to be echoing Angelina's own
thoughts earlier in the day, she looked at him wide-
eyed. Then she said:

79

"Please, let me help. It seems absurd that I might be ... able to do so ... and yet sometimes we are helped in ways we do not ... expect."

"As I did not expect you."

The Prince looked at her for a moment, then said:

"Very well, let me start at the beginning. My family have been the heriditary Rulers of Cephalonia for hundreds of years, although of course the seven Ionian islands have been colonised many times in their history."

"First they were under the protection of Venice," Angelina murmured.

The Prince smiled, as if he was pleased that she was so knowledgeable.

"Then the French," he said, "followed by the English, but your country gave Cephalonia back to us in 1864."

"And now you must keep it," Angelina said positively.

"That is, of course, what I feel," the Prince agreed, "and my Cousin Theodoros Vlachos is fanatical on the subject."

He paused for a moment, then went on:

"It was only at the end of my father's reign and now in mine that there were any difficulties and some people wished to surrender our Royal independence to the Government in Athens."

"You must not do that," Angelina said quickly.

"It will not be easy to prevent it," the Prince replied, "and yet it is difficult to understand why this revolutionary spirit, this dissension, has suddenly arisen."

He was silent for a moment, as if he was thinking over what had occurred, then he said:

"You may perhaps have wondered why, since we are such a small country, we have such an impressive Ministry."

"Grandmama said she was surprised when she first learnt who had come next door."

"That was due to one of my own relatives," the

Prince said. "Our family name is Vlachos, and there are a large number of them in Cephalonia, but my Cousin Theodoros Vlachos is rather different from the others."

"In what way?" Angelina enquired.

"Because," the Prince explained, "he is an extremely rich man. He first made a lot of money abroad in shipping. Then when he came home, he was afraid that our island might lose our own Government and our own Ruling House, although of course we are Greeks and we acknowledge King George I."

There was something in the way the Prince said the King's name which made Angelina remember that George I was Danish, not Greek.

It was, she recalled, the British who had secured the election of Prince William George of Holstein-Glucksburg, son of the King of Denmark, to the Greek throne.

It was after his accession as George I that the Ionic islands were ceded to Greece by the British.

"Why does your Cousin feel so strongly about this?" Angelina enquired.

"Mostly because of the trouble in Crete. Theodoros was horrified that the King's second son should have become High Commissioner under the Sultan, and he is terrified that the same thing might happen in Cephalonia."

"I can understand his feelings," Angelina murmured.

"He has therefore persuaded a number of European powers, including Britain, to recognise Cephalonia as an independent part of Greece."

The Prince smiled as he added:

"It was my Cousin who built the new Cephalonian Ministry, something my Government could not have afforded."

The Prince paused for a moment, then said:

"It is also my Cousin who is anxious for me to marry. He and the Prime Minister are convinced that it could disperse the revolutionary element on the island."

81

"Do all your Statesmen agree?" Angelina asked.

"The majority of them follow where the Prime Minister leads. There is, however, one who is against it."

"Who is that?" Angelina asked, feeling she must show an intelligent interest in what he was saying.

"A man called Kharilaos Costas," the Prince replied. "He is the Foreign Minister, and will be arriving at the Ministry tonight."

"And he does not wish you to marry?"

"No; he was violently against it from the very beginning," the Prince replied. "I do not like the man, but I respect his views on this particular subject."

He spoke almost to himself, then he looked at Angelina and added:

"It is a rather complicated story, but then, as you know, all Greek stories are. There is a great deal more I could tell you, but that is the broad outline."

"What it really amounts to," Angelina said, "is that your Cousin, whom you obviously cannot afford to offend, wants you to marry and make quite certain your Royal heritage is not swept away by a revolutionary group."

"That is putting it in a nut-shell," the Prince agreed, "and the only person who suffers is me!"

"You ... may find ... someone you love," Angelina suggested.

"I have!" the Prince answered. "But I cannot marry her!"

There was an almost frightening silence.

Then as Angelina's eyes met his, he said very quietly:

"I fell in love the moment I saw you!"

# Chapter Four

"It ... is not ... true!" Angelina said in a frightened little voice.

"It is true!" the Prince answered. "When I saw you standing in the Hall it was as if a light enveloped you."

He paused for a moment, looking at Angelina in a way which made her tremble, then said:

"The air of Cephalonia quivers with a brilliant yet soft light which is famous all over Greece. I had never seen it anywhere else in the world, until I saw you."

"H-how can you ... say things like ... that?" Angelina asked, almost beneath her breath.

"You are so beautiful," the Prince said, "so exactly what I have been looking for all my life, and now, when I have found you, I can do nothing about it."

There was a throb of pain in his voice which made Angelina want to put out her hands towards him.

She could not bear him to suffer. She could not bear to think that she was making him unhappy.

"It is agony to look at you," he went on, "agony to know that you can never be mine, and yet in a way it is a wonder beyond words to know that you exist, to know that there is someone like the goddesses in whom I have believed all my life."

Angelina clasped her hands together.

The Prince's voice seemed to vibrate through her

and she felt her whole being respond to it, as if not she but he was the light of Apollo which draws all human beings with its brilliance.

She knew, because she had read about it so often, that light meant more to the Greeks than to any other people in the world.

As if once again the Prince knew what she was thinking, he said:

"Homer described the Goddess Athene as the 'bright-eyed one,' and Helen as wearing a 'shining veil.' To me, you are encircled with that same light— the light which is so intense and so pure that it comes from the very heat of the sun."

Angelina could only look at him, transfixed by what he was saying. She had never thought, never imagined, that anyone could speak to her in such a way, let alone the Prince.

"I love you!" he went on. "I love you until nothing else seems of any importance, and yet what can I do?"

It was a cry that seemed to come from the depths of his being, and as Angelina responded to it with her heart, her brain told her that she had to help him and she was the one who must be strong.

It is she who must tell him what he had to do and strengthen him to do his duty towards his country.

She clasped her hands together for fear that without her conscious volition they should reach out to touch him.

Then she said:

"Whatever we ... feel for each ... other, Cephalonia ... must come ... first."

"*We* feel for each other?" the Prince repeated. "Tell me, my lovely little Persephone, what you feel for me."

His tone was insistent, demanding, and Angelina could not look at him.

"Tell me," he said again.

For a moment she hesitated, and then, because she

knew he was waiting, because she was still acutely conscious that he was suffering, she whispered:

"I ... love you!"

He shut his eyes for a second, as if he could not bear the beauty of her face or the softness in her eyes when she spoke the words he wanted to hear.

Before he could speak, Angelina went on:

"But as you say, there is nothing we can do about it. You have to marry the ... right person who will save Cephalonia from the ... revolutionaries."

"I know that is what I must do," the Prince said in a dull voice. "But what about you? What will happen to you, Angelina?"

She did not answer, and he continued:

"You will marry—of course you will marry—but I cannot bear to think of it."

Angelina did not reply, but she thought it was unlikely that she would ever find anyone who would wish to marry her, and so she would spend the rest of her many years alone in her grandmother's house.

She would be surrounded by old people and have no-one to talk to except Twi-Twi.

"For my peace of mind," the Prince said, as if he followed her train of thought, "it is easier to think of you reading in bed, tending your grandmother, and walking in the garden alone with your dog—except that perhaps another man will meet you there, as I did."

"If I met a ... hundred men," Angelina said, "none would be like ... you."

It was true, she thought as she said it. There could never be anyone like the Prince, and not only because he was so handsome and, with his square shoulders and dark eloquent eyes, so different from any other man she had seen before.

But there was also, she knew, a magnetic link between them which had been there from the very first moment when she had turned round in the Hall, with

Twi-Twi in her arms, to find him standing in front of her.

Their eyes had met and she had felt something strange happen to her heart.

She had not realised it at the time, but now she thought that it was the moment when the arrow of love had pierced her, and nothing could ever be the same again.

She remembered too the little shaft of lightning which she had felt flash through her body when the Prince had touched her hand.

She had experienced the same feeling when he had turned her round in the carriage so that she should not look at the deocrations but at him.

'We belong,' she thought to herself.

She thought that if it was an agony for him to leave her, it would be even worse for her to lose him.

He would have other things in his life—his country, his people, the endless duties which must concern a Ruler, and of course the necessity of finding a wife.

She felt as if her whole being cried out at the thought of him married to somebody else; to a woman who, even if she grew to care for him, would never love him in the same way as she did.

It was not only that their bodies vibrated to each other and that their minds were attuned in a manner which made him know what she was thinking, in the same way that she could be perceptive and understanding about him.

"If I were an ordinary man," the Prince said now, "and had met you at a Ball or in the garden because we were both living in the same Square, would you marry me?"

"You ... know the answer to ... that question," Angelina replied, "but we must not ... think about it ... because it will only make us ... unhappy."

"Am I making you unhappy?" the Prince asked.

Angelina looked at him and he saw the answer in her eyes.

"It is wrong and cruel of me!" he exclaimed. "I wanted to bring you happiness, to make this a perfect evening for you to remember, as I shall remember it."

He gave a deep sigh.

"I told myself when I was dressing, and looking forward so impatiently to seeing you again, that I would not tell you of my true feelings. We would laugh and talk, and it would be a night of gladness—nothing else."

He sighed again.

"But when you came to me, looking so beautiful with flowers in your hair, all my resolutions flew away as if on wings, and I only wanted to speak to you of my love."

"It is . . . something I shall . . . always remember," Angelina said.

The Prince suddenly brought his fist down hard on the table, making her start and the coffee-cups rattle.

"Do not speak like that!" he said fiercely. "You are putting everything in the past-tense. We still have the present—this moment, tonight, tomorrow, the day after, until I am forced to return to Cephalonia."

Angelina turned her face away from him to look at the Restaurant, but she did not see the people dining there or the waiters moving amongst the tables.

She saw only the emptiness and the quietness of the house where she lived and what it would be like when there was no-one of any interest to look at next door and no-one waiting for her in the garden.

"Whatever happens in the . . . future," she said bravely, "as you have said, we shall always have . . . this to remember . . . and I could never . . . forget."

"Nor could I," the Prince answered. "I realise I have been vouchsafed a glimpse of Heaven, which few men have in their lifetime."

He smiled, but it was merely a bitter twist of his lips.

"I came to England full of resentment and anger," he said, "because I expected that while I was here I would be obliged to meet the woman I was to marry for political reasons."

He made a gesture with his hands as he went on:

"Then what happened? I thought I had left behind everything that meant anything to me, the light of Greece, glittering, transparent, quivering, which I thought was not to be found anywhere else in the world, until I saw you!"

"Did I ... really seem to shine with ... a light?" Angelina asked.

"To me it was blindingly clear," the Prince answered. "The light in you was that which the Ancient Greeks believed made their eyes see farther and gave their bodies unsuspected powers."

"You ... could not ... say anything more ... wonderful to me."

She thought, as she spoke, that she might tell the Prince her secret.

Then it struck her that he might be shocked, or perhaps it would detract from her some of the light with which he now saw her surrounded.

It was what she had longed for and what sometimes she felt she could see in the stars overhead and in the glimmer of water, and which was at times translated into music like a light in her ears.

Because she had read so much about Greece and its ancient mysteries, she understood exactly what the Prince was saying to her.

His tone of voice and the look in his eyes told her he was not just paying her a compliment but was speaking with a sincerity that came from the very depths of his heart.

Yet what he was saying astonished her.

The light of Greece and the glory of the gods were

# A Personal Invitation from Barbara Cartland

Dear Reader,

I have formed the Barbara Cartland "Health and Happiness Club" so that I can share with you my sensational discoveries on beauty, health, love and romance, which is both physical and spiritual.

I will communicate with you through a series of newsletters throughout the year which will serve as a forum for you to tell me what you personally have felt, and you will also be able to learn the thoughts and feelings of other members who join me in my "Search for Rainbows." I will be thrilled to know you wish to participate.

In addition, the Health and Happiness Club will make available to members only, the finest quality health and beauty care products personally selected by me.

Do please join my Health and Happiness Club. Together we will find the secrets which bring rapture and ecstasy to my heroines and point the way to true happiness.

Yours,

# FREE Membership Offer

# Health
# &
# Happiness Club

Dear Barbara,

Please enroll me as a charter member in the Barbara Cartland "Health and Happiness Club." My membership application appears on the form below (or on a plain piece of paper).

I look forward to receiving the first in a series of your newsletters and learning about your sensational discoveries on beauty, health, love and romance.

I understand that the newsletters and membership in your club are _free_.

\* \* \*

Kindly send your membership application to:
Health and Happiness Club, Inc.
Two Penn Plaza
New York, N.Y. 10001

NAME_____

ADDRESS_____

CITY_____STATE____ZIP_____

Allow 2 weeks for delivery of the first newsletter.

all hidden secretly within her mind. She had never spoken of them to anyone and thought it unlikely that she would ever be able to do so.

Even when she had imagined, as other girls did, that one day she would fall in love, she had never dreamt that she would be able to talk to her husband of such things, knowing that an Englishman like her father would not understand.

He either would have laughed at her for being childish or would have been suspicious that she was not normal or in fact slightly freakish.

But the Prince not only understood, he went further, and it occurred to Angelina that she could have learnt from him so many things that she herself could not understand.

But now there would be no time to hear them.

"What can we do?" the Prince asked, breaking in on her thoughts. "What can we do, Angelina? God knows I cannot imagine life without you."

"You will have ... Cephalonia," Angelina replied, "and we are really of little ... importance beside the safety of your ... mountainous Paradise."

"My people suffered so severely under the Turks," the Prince said, "it must never happen again."

"Of course not," Angelina said quickly. "But I understand that the Germans favour the Turks."

She saw the darkness and anger in the Prince's expression and wished she had kept silent.

"The Turks are still a menace to us," he said, "and the Germans are jealous of your power and your colonies."

"I know."

"So much hatred, so little love."

As he spoke the Prince put his hand out towards Angelina, and, knowing what he wanted, she laid her own hand in his.

She felt again the shaft of lightning sweep through her, which was very wonderful.

"I love you!" the Prince said in his deep voice. "And because I love you so overwhelmingly, my darling, I will do nothing to hurt you—nothing, if I can help it, that will make you unhappy."

"It will be ... agony when I have to ... lose you," Angelina said, "but I shall always be grateful that I have ... known how ... wonderful a man can be."

There was a little sob that she could not prevent in her words, and the Prince's fingers tightened on hers. Then he took his hand away and said:

"We have a little more time together—tonight I am taking you to see the decorations and tomorrow I am going to ask you to dine with me again."

"But I thought you said you had an ... engagement which you could not ... break," Angelina said.

"I am not going to break it," the Prince answered. "I am going to take you with me."

Angelina waited and he went on:

"There are quite a number of Cephalonians in London. They are all working people who meet every month in a Restaurant where one can eat Greek food."

He smiled as he said:

"We shall have a very different meal from what we have had here tonight, but I want you to meet some of the Cephalonians over whom I reign."

"Will they want to meet me?" Angelina asked.

"They will be proud to meet any friend of mine," the Prince answered, "and particularly somebody as beautiful as you. There is not a Greek living who does not appreciate beauty when he sees it."

"May I ... really come with you?"

"I would not ask you to do so if I thought there was any danger," the Prince replied. "But these people need not know who you are, and you are very unlikely to meet them in the Society in which you and your grandmother move."

He went on:

"You will eat the food that you would eat if you

were with me in Cephalonia and you will see how my people dance when they are happy or when they celebrate."

It flashed through Angelina's mind that it was the way they would dance at his marriage, and as if he thought the same thing the Prince said quickly:

"When we are apart it will make us seem closer, if you know the way I am living, and I am selfish enough, Angelina, to want you not to forget me."

"I could ... never do that," she replied, "and if you think it is ... right for me to do so, I would love to come with you tomorrow night."

"Then we will go together," the Prince said, a smile illuminating his face, "and perhaps we can meet in the morning for a few minutes in the garden, but you must not be disappointed, as I shall be, if I am unable to come."

"What will you be doing?" she asked.

"As my Foreign Minister is arriving tonight and he has been visiting a number of European countries," the Prince answered, "we shall have a long and doubtless very boring meeting at which he will talk interminably about the conferences in which he has been involved."

"Why do you not like this man?" Angelina asked curiously.

The Prince knitted his brows.

"I do not know exactly, and it is very indiscreet of me to admit to you that I dislike him," he answered, "but there is something wrong about him, which I cannot quite put my finger on, and yet it is there."

"I know that feeling exactly," Angelina said, "and I am sure that one should always trust one's intuition."

"I would trust yours anywhere," the Prince replied, "and I like to trust my own. But you know as well as I do that nowadays people expect dossiers, reports, references, and personal histories before they make up their minds about a fellow human being."

"Papa has told me how intuitive the people are in

India. Although he did not say so, I know that some Indians can see the aura of a person to whom they are talking, and others have a clairvoyant insight which is never at fault."

"I do not have to be clairvoyant to know that everything about you is perfect," the Prince said. "It radiates from you in a light which haloes you as it haloed Apollo when he leapt from a ship disguised as a star at high noon."

Angelina gave a little cry of delight and added:

"The flames shone round him and a flash of splendour lit the sky."

"Then the star vanished," the Prince continued, "and there was only a handsome young man armed with a bow and arrows."

Angelina clapped her hands together.

"You have read the same story!"

"It is the most beloved one in the whole history of the gods," the Prince answered. "It was then that Apollo chose the place for his Temple at Delphi."

"You have been there?"

"Of course! Many times."

"It is where I long to go," Angelina said. "Did you feel Apollo near you when you stood beneath the Shining Cliffs?"

"I felt a kind of quietness and saw the light above and below me," the Prince answered. "But I felt alone. I know now it was because you were not with me."

"Perhaps one day I shall be able to come to Greece," Angelina said in a dreamy voice.

"Do you think it would give me any pleasure to know that you were there without me?" the Prince asked.

He made a sound that was almost a cry.

"I want to be with you in Greece, Angelina. There is so much I want to show you, so much that I can talk to you about, so much that we can feel together."

Her eyes were irresistibly drawn to his and he looked deep into them and said:

"How can I be without you? How can I live, knowing that you are somewhere in the world but I cannot see or touch you?"

"When you ... talk like that," Angelina said, "you make things ... worse."

"But not as bad as they will be," the Prince answered. "When I came to England I was longing to return to Cephalonia, but now when I leave, only a part of me will go home. My heart will stay with you."

Their eyes held each other's until the Prince, with what was almost a superhuman effort, looked away and said in a voice that was suddenly harsh:

"I must not keep you out too late."

He asked for the bill, and when it was paid they rose without speaking and Angelina led the way out of the Restaurant.

The Head Waiter bowed obsequiously at the door and the Prince thanked him for an excellent dinner, but Angelina knew that neither of them had tasted what they had eaten.

Outside, the carriage was waiting for them. Alexis had Twi-Twi sitting beside him on the box.

He handed the small white Pekingese to the Prince, who helped Angelina into the carriage, then put Twi-Twi on the seat opposite her.

The hood had been opened as he had promised, and while they had been in the Restaurant, darkness had come, and now the gas-lamps threw a golden glow all down the street.

They drove into Piccadilly and Angelina could see that most of the shops had illuminated decorations which shone brightly on the flags, the bunting, and the portraits of the new King and Queen.

It made the streets of London look very gay and somehow swept away a lot of their sombre dignity, so that they had quite a raffish air.

Angelina looked round her with delight. Then she felt the Prince take her hand in his, and as if she could not help herself, she drew a little closer to him.

"It is just how I thought it would look," she said in an excited voice, "and it seems right that there should also be a moon and stars in the sky."

She looked up as she spoke, and the Prince, seeing her thrown-back head and the exquisite line of her neck, drew in his breath.

Alexis drove them through Piccadilly Circus, then down the Haymarket and into Trafalgar Square.

The fountains, illuminated with concealed lights, were throwing iridescent rainbows high into the sky. There were garlands round Nelson's Column, and flags and bunting round every lamp-post.

There was the sound of a hurdy-gurdy and some young people were dancing round it while a crowd watched and applauded.

"You see how happy everyone is that your King is well enough to be crowned?" the Prince remarked.

"He is very popular," Angelina replied, "and they call him 'Edward the Peacemaker.'"

"Let us hope he can keep the peace," the Prince remarked.

Angelina knew that he was thinking that the Germans might be a menace to Great Britain as the Turks still menaced the Greeks.

She turned towards him impulsively.

"Let us forget politics for the next few days," she begged," and perhaps too we could forget the ... future."

"Forget that we have to part?" the Prince asked.

"Yes. After all, we are so lucky to have the present. Please ... please do not let us miss a single moment of it."

"All right," he agreed, "and there is always the chance that tomorrow may never come."

"Even if it does," Angelina said, "we shall have had ... today."

"You are very wise, my little Persephone."

As he spoke, he raised her hand and kissed it.

There was something in the touch of his lips on her skin that made her quiver with a thousand feelings she had never known before.

"Oh, God, I love you so much!" the Prince cried. "I promise, my lovely one, that I will try to make the present, for us both, as perfect as it is possible for it to be."

The carriage drove through Admiralty Arch and into the Mall.

Here the decorations on the lamp-posts were dignified and yet attractive, but Angelina's eyes went to where the moon was shining on the lake in St. James's Park.

She could see the glimmer of silver between the trees and she thought that it looked very romantic and very entrancing.

The Prince's eyes were on her face.

"Shall we go and look at the ducks?" he asked. "My guide-book tells me they were first introduced there by your 'Merrie Monarch'—Charles II."

"Can we ... do that?"

"Why not?"

He called out to Alexis, who drew the horse to a standstill.

"We will leave you to look after the little dog," the Prince said. "We will not be long."

He put his arm under Angelina's and she pulled her velvet wrap round her shoulders, thinking that perhaps she looked too smart to be walking in the Park, as if she were a country sight-seer.

But the crowds who had been wandering there earlier in the day had gone home to bed, and there was only an occasional couple close to each other in the shadows of the trees.

When they reached the bridge over the lake, they were alone in an enchanted place, for the moon turned everything to silver, even themselves.

Angelina was acutely conscious that the Prince's eyes had been on her face as they had walked along together, but there seemed nothing to say.

Or rather, they had talked to each other without words, knowing a strange, almost overwhelming contentment because they were close and because his hand was touching her bare arm.

They stood as if looking at the ducks, but there were none to be seen. Then as they turned to walk back again towards the carriage, the Prince stopped under the shadowy branches of a tree.

Angelina looked up at him enquiringly and he spoke for the first time since they had left the carriage.

"I want to kiss you," he said, "I want it more than I have ever wanted anything in my whole life, but if you tell me I should not do so, then I will obey you, because I love you too much to do anything that you would not wish."

Angelina did not answer.

She only looked up at him, and though neither of them seemed to move, she was close in his arms and he was holding her tightly against him.

Then as her eyes were still held by his, he bent his head and his lips found hers.

It was a very gentle kiss, the kiss of a man who touches something so sacred that he is half-afraid that he is committing sacrilege.

Angelina's mouth was very soft beneath his, and as his kiss deepened, a wonder that seemed to come from the sky itself drew them together with a divine radiance.

Angelina felt as if light were quivering round them and they were one with the shining stars, the silver glimmer of water, and the soft music that came from within their souls.

It was so perfect, and she felt as if she touched the very wings of ecstasy and was lifted into the sky itself.

Then there came a little flicker of fire which she had never known before.

It seemed to rise from the very depths of her body, through her breasts, and into her lips, and to join with the fire which she felt burning in the Prince and which held all the mystery and wonder of the divine.

It might have spanned the centuries and been part of the same flames which had soared from Apollo and made him appear as if he were a star.

It was impossible to determine how long their kiss lasted.

The Prince raised his head, and Angelina, looking up at him, felt as if they had both ceased to exist as human beings and had been transfigured into gods.

For one moment they were still, and then, because there were no words to express what they felt, they walked quietly hand-in-hand back towards the carriage.

As Alexis drove on, their hands were clasped, and only when they came down Grosvenor Crescent and reached the Square, turning not towards the front of the houses but to the Mews at the back, did the Prince say, in a voice that was curiously unlike his own:

"If I do not see you before tomorrow evening, I will be waiting at the same time as tonight."

The carriage came to a standstill outside the garden door.

The Prince drew the key from the cushioning where he had placed it, and then as Angelina picked up Twi-Twi in her arms, he helped her out of the carriage and opened the door which led into the garden.

When he had done so, he put the key in her hand, and as she quivered at the touch of him she looked up into his eyes.

The moonlight was on their faces and for a long, long moment they stared at each other.

"Good-night, my precious love," the Prince said hoarsely.

"Good . . . night," Angelina whispered.

She passed through the garden door and he shut it behind her. Then with feet that hardly seemed to touch the ground she ran to the door of the house.

She let herself in, put the key to the outer door back into the dish from which she had taken it, then put Twi-Twi down on the ground because it was easier in the darkness of the house to find her way if she could hold out both her hands in front of her.

Only when she reached her bed-room could she think, and she knew that what had happened tonight was as wonderful and mystic as if she had taken part in the mysteries of Eleusis.

She felt that tonight she had really been Persephone. But she had not handed the symbolic ear of corn to an initiate who had passed through all the terrors of the underworld, but had herself received the sacred token.

She sat down on the edge of her bed.

'This is love,' she thought, 'the love that is so perfect, so truly part of God, that, having once known it, one could never contemplate an imitation.'

She knew then that when she lost the Prince it would be impossible for her ever to marry anybody else.

How could she give any other man what she had given him—not only her heart but her soul?

She knew, without his telling her in words, that what she had experienced, he had experienced too.

It had been as if they had been encircled by a special light quivering and beating in the air, and the wings of the gods had swept them up into the sky and nothing could ever be the same again.

At the moment, Angelina did not even think of how she would suffer when she lost the Prince.

She was only worshipping at the shrine to which their love had taken them, knowing that she had been sanctified and blessed above all other women.

* * *

When old Emily came into her bed-room the next morning, Angelina felt as if she had only just fallen asleep.

She had lain awake pulsating with the wonder of the Prince's lips, feeling that she was still in his arms, still lifted into the skies, enveloped by the light of the gods.

"It's a nice sunny day, Miss Angelina," Emily said in her croaking old voice as she pulled back the curtains, "and you mark my words, it'll be fine tomorrow for the Coronation."

"Would you like to watch the King arrive at Buckingham Palace, Emily?" Angelina asked, sitting up in bed.

"I'm too old for that sort of thing," Emily replied. "I'll read about it in the newspapers. Although I'd like to see the King and Queen with my own eyes, my feet wouldn't carry me there."

It had just been an idea, Angelina thought with a little sigh, that perhaps she could persuade Emily at the very last minute to go with her into the crowds.

She knew, however, that if she was honest it was not the King and Queen she wanted to see, but the Prince. But after all, she could have a private view of him from the garden.

He would look very handsome in his uniform with all his decorations, she thought, though it did not matter at all what he wore.

It was his eyes that she wanted to see, and the expression in them when he looked at her, which told her even better than words that he loved her as she loved him.

"Could any man be more wonderful, more magnificent?" she asked herself.

And she knew, as she had last night, that it would be impossible for any other man to mean anything in her life.

He had said that he might be able to get away and meet her in the garden, and because every nerve in her body longed to see him and be with him, Angelina dressed so quickly that she was downstairs before Ruston was ready for her.

"You're very early, Miss Angelina!" he said. "I doubt as your egg's cooked yet."

"It does not matter," Angelina answered. "I am not hungry."

"You must have a proper breakfast," old Ruston said firmly. "We can't have you looking thin like the General."

He went off slowly down the stairs to the kitchen and Angelina waited, knowing that there would be a terrible fuss if she did not eat any breakfast, but feeling as if every second that kept her from the garden was a century of drawn-out time.

She took Twi-Twi for only a short walk immediately after breakfast and before she went to her grandmother's room, and then for a longer walk after she had read aloud the headline news in the papers and helped Lady Medwin to open her letters.

There were usually not many of these.

At the same time, there were bills and demands for charity, which if they were urgent, Angelina either paid or answered without waiting for Miss Musgrove.

She was an elderly secretary whom her grandmother had employed for years, and she came in on Fridays to pay the household wages and do all the other clerical jobs which seemed to accumulate unless they were attended to regularly.

At last Ruston came into the Dining-Room, carrying a tray on which reposed a silver coffee-pot, a silver cream-jug, and a covered dish which contained a poached egg and two slices of bacon, which Angelina was expected to eat for breakfast.

There was also a toast-rack with four slices of toast, and it took him a long time to set everything down on the table.

This had already been laid with a silver tray, a cup and saucer, plates, a pat of golden butter, a fresh comb of honey, and a glass jar containing marmalade.

Everything was in its place, as it had been for years, and would continue to be in the years ahead, Angelina thought.

Then she wondered how many years she would have to wait before the Prince paid another visit to England.

Would he come for the wedding of one of the Princesses? Or perhaps for the funeral of the new King?

She felt almost ashamed of thinking that the King might die, and yet he had not come to the throne until he was sixty-five, and considering the way he indulged himself, there was no reason to anticipate that he would live as long as his mother, Queen Victoria, had done.

She should not want to see the Prince in such sad circumstances, Angelina chided herself.

Then she thought that whatever the circumstances, she would want to see him, but she might still have to wait years and years to do so.

It was a depressing thought, and Angelina remembered that she herself had suggested that they should live in the present and try to ignore the future.

'It is the only thing we can do,' she thought, knowing that otherwise they would tear themselves to pieces emotionally when they had to say good-bye.

Already at the thought, deep within herself a voice

was crying: 'How can I bear it? How can I bear it?' but she would not listen.

She ate what she could of the breakfast, just to please Ruston.

Then she ran up the stairs to her grandmother's room, followed by Twi-Twi, who had been sitting under the table while she ate.

"You are very early, dearest," Lady Medwin said, "and how pretty you look this morning!"

"Thank you, Grandmama. Did you have a good night?"

"A very good night, as it happens," Lady Medwin answered. "It must have been because I had a rest yesterday afternoon. Dear Sir William always knows what is best for me, and I must try to do the same today."

"Yes, of course, Grandmama," Angelina agreed. "And if I look pretty, so do you!"

Lady Medwin smiled.

She never slept very late in the morning, and already she had on a bed-jacket of pink satin trimmed with frills of lace and she wore one of her becoming little caps, this one threaded with coral-pink ribbons, which was quite coquettish.

"Only two boring letters this morning," Lady Medwin said, looking at them where they lay on her bed, "so tell me if there is any excitement in the newspapers. Then you must take Twi-Twi to the garden."

With an effort Angelina found the few headlines that interested her grandmother, then because she could bear it no longer she said:

"I really think Twi-Twi should go out, Grandmama."

"Then take him," Lady Medwin said, "and when you come back I want you to see if there is a description of the Ball at Devonshire House last night. It sounded as if it was going to be very impressive, and I expect our young neighbour, Prince Xenos, was there."

Angelina could not remember anything she had read to her grandmother yesterday morning, and because the mere sound of the Prince's name brought the blood rushing to her cheeks, she said a little incoherently:

"Why ... should you think the ... Prince was there ... Grandmama?"

"Because the Ball was obviously given for all the Royalty who have arrived for the Coronation," Lady Medwin said, a note of reproof in her voice, as if she thought Angelina was being rather stupid.

"Yes ... yes ... of course."

"Anyway, we will find his name amongst the list of guests when you come back," Lady Medwin said. "I feel I have been rather remiss in not calling at the Ministry next door, but it is only one of the many things I have been unable to do since I have been ill."

"You will soon be well, Grandmama," Angelina said optimistically, "and the first thing we will do will be to call at the Cephalonian Ministry."

She reached the door as she spoke and turned back to say:

"As it is so near, we shall not need the carriage to carry us there."

"Not need the carriage?" Lady Medwin exclaimed. "I never heard of such a thing! Of course we will call properly. The Minister would think it very strange if we arrived on foot."

Angelina did not reply, but she was smiling as she went downstairs at such a speed that Twi-Twi could hardly keep up with her.

It was so like her grandmother, she thought, to do everything in the conventional and prescribed manner.

Then she wondered what Lady Medwin would say if she knew how unconventional her granddaughter had been in dining alone with a man last night, and the Prince at that, and hurrying now to meet him in the garden.

103

"Please, God," she prayed, "let Grandmama never find out."

She had left her hat in the Hall when she came down to breakfast, and now she put it on her head, having a quick glance at herself in the gilt-framed mirror which stood above the table on which there was a silver salver waiting to hold the cards of those who called.

There were only a few cards there now, which were looking rather dilapidated because they had been there for so long.

Almost for the first time, as she looked at it Angelina did not regret that her grandmother was ill and therefore, as they could make no calls in return, very few people called on them.

It seemed unkind, but if Lady Medwin had been well, Angelina would never have met the Prince as she had, and certainly not have been able to be with him last night.

It had all been so marvellous, so unlike anything she had ever imagined would happen to her, and certainly it was something which should *not* have happened.

But that was what made it such an adventure, and that, Angelina thought, was perhaps why she must pay for such enchantment with a broken heart.

Ruston handed her the key to the garden, asking her, as usual, if she was going out.

Then she was speeding across the road to let herself in through the gate.

She had not expected the Prince to be there so early, but even so, her heart sank because the garden was empty.

She walked slowly across the lawn, willing him to come and join her, willing him to be aware that she was waiting for him, wanting him.

Twi-Twi was frisking round as he usually did first thing in the morning, and Angelina sat down on the wooden seat under the trees in the centre of the garden and waited.

"If I shut my eyes," she told herself, "and then open them quickly, I shall see him coming towards me."

She felt the excitement rise within her at the thought, and it seemed like the little flame of last night that had risen in her throat now rose to her lips.

She knew it was part of the divine power of love, which she had read about but never thought to experience.

She had not really understood what the words meant until last night, when the sensation had been there and the ecstasy and rapture she had found when the Prince kissed her.

'I love you! I love you!' she said in her heart, then opened her eyes, feeling that he must be coming to her.

But there was only the sunshine and Twi-Twi.

Otherwise the garden was empty....

# Chapter Five

It was childish to be so disappointed, Angelina told herself, but all through the morning there was a heavy stone in her breast and it would not move away.

When she went back into the garden later with Twi-Twi, she knew that the Prince had said he had meetings all day and so it would be impossible for him to join her.

At the same time, nothing could prevent her eyes from turning in the direction of the gate, just in case he should come walking in.

At luncheon she ate alone as usual; then, after her grandmother had settled herself for her long rest, Angelina once again went rather forlornly into the garden.

It seemed strange that today the sunshine was not so golden, and she did not want to play with Twi-Twi or do anything but sit on the seat and think about last night.

She deliberately recaptured the magic of the Prince's kiss and the emotions he had evoked in her, which made her feel that they were no longer human but gods.

And yet as she did so, she had the terrifying feeling that even the memory of what she had experienced was slipping away into the past. In time it would grow dim, and like a faded photograph would arouse no sensation but that of wistful nostalgia.

Yet as she thought such things, she knew that her imagination was once again running riot and she could not control it.

She wanted the Prince so acutely, and longed for him with an urgency which in its very violence seemed to leave her weak and limp.

She found herself calculating how many hours and minutes there were not only before this evening, when she would see him again, but before he left England.

She knew that however much he might wish to stay on at the Ministry, it would cause comment for him to do so when there were difficulties in his own country and doubtless a thousand decisions awaiting his return.

She was well aware, because it had been reported in the newspapers, that most of the other Kings and Queens who were attending the Coronation would leave immediately after it.

There was nothing, she told herself with a wry little smile, more boring than a guest who would not depart.

So the Prince would return to his own country and there would only be the flag outside the Cephalonian Ministry to remind her of him.

"I love him! I love him!" she cried.

As she left the garden, she looked up the street at the impressive front door and the six white steps down which the Prince would walk when he left the Ministry.

She wondered if he was thinking of her and felt somehow that their thoughts of each other met between the two houses.

"I love you!" she whispered again, thinking that perhaps the soft breeze which had just stirred the flag might carry her words to him in the Council Chamber, or wherever he was sitting.

Her grandmother was waiting for her, looking refreshed, having slept the prescribed two hours.

"And today," she told Angelina proudly, "without taking Sir William's soothing draught."

"You look very pretty, Grandmama!" Angelina said, picking up *The Times* and turning to the Social Column.

She had just found the Duke and Duchess of Devonshire's name above the long list of distinguished guests, when there was a knock on the door and old Ruston entered the room.

He was breathless from the stairs, but he managed to announce:

"Lady Hewlett, My Lady!"

Angelina rose to her feet.

Lady Hewlett was a very old friend of her grandmother's and Lady Medwin was always talking about her.

She too had been very good-looking in her youth, but now she tried to recapture the years she had lost by dying her hair and wearing a very obvious amount of powder and rouge.

This would have been considered outrageous and very fast in anyone younger or less distinguished, but Lord Hewlett had been the British Ambassador in some of the important Capitals of Europe and Lady Hewlett was a law unto herself.

"Lily, dearest," she said now to Lady Medwin, holding out both her hands and rustling towards her, exuding the fragrance of expensive French perfume.

"Daisy, what a surprise!" Lady Medwin exclaimed. "I saw in the newspapers that you were in England, but I did not expect you to have time to call and see me until after the Coronation."

"I found I had a few hours to spare this afternoon, so I have been calling on my old friends," Lady Hewlett explained. "But why are you in bed?"

109

"I have not been well for some months," Lady Medwin replied, "and it has been very tiresome of me to be ill this summer of all summers, when I should have been presenting Angelina and taking her to all the important Balls."

"I heard that Angelina had not yet made her curtsey at Buckingham Palace," Lady Hewlett said, "but why did you not let me know, Lily? I would have presented her myself."

Lady Medwin made a sound that was curiously like a groan.

"Why did I not think of that?" she exclaimed. "But quite frankly, Daisy, I did not expect you to be in England."

"I had no intention of missing the Coronation," Lady Hewlett said, "and neither had Arthur, and of course we have a special place in the Abbey where we shall see everything beautifully!"

"How I envy you," Lady Medwin said with a sigh.

Lady Hewlett seated herself in the chair near the bed and looked at Angelina, who picked up the newspapers and was preparing to leave the room. Her shrewd eyes missed nothing, and after a moment she said:

"You have grown very pretty, Angelina. Very pretty indeed! You must come and stay with me in Paris, and I know all the glamorous young Frenchmen will go into ecstasies over you."

"It is ... very kind of you to think of it," Angelina replied.

She was sure in her own mind that Lady Hewlett would forget the invitation once she had left England.

"That reminds me," Lady Hewlett said, "I am giving a party to which I had intended, Lily, to invite both you and Angelina, but if you cannot come, you must allow your granddaughter to come alone. I will look after her."

Angelina drew in her breath.

If Lady Hewlett's party was for tonight she could not go.

But, she thought frantically, how could she say so? How could she possibly explain that she had another engagement?

She held her breath in sheer terror as Lady Hewlett went on:

"It is only a small party—about thirty people to dinner and about the same number coming in afterwards, but I thought it would be amusing to have a Band so that we could dance."

She gave Lady Medwin what was almost a coy look as she added:

"I thought, until I went to Paris, that my dancing days were over, but the French convinced me otherwise."

"Your party sounds delightful!" Lady Medwin said. "But I know my Doctors would not hear of my attempting anything so strenuous."

"Then your pretty Angelina must come without you." Lady Hewlett answered. "I will send the carriage for her and a maid to accompany her, if you do not like her to drive alone."

"You are very kind!" Lady Medwin said with a smile. "And Angelina has some very charming gowns, so you will not be ashamed of her appearance."

"She will be the Belle of the evening!" Lady Hewlett said. "And I must think where else I can take her while I am in London."

"Daisy, you are kindness itself!" Lady Medwin enthused. "I have always told you, Angelina, have I not, that there is no-one with such a warm heart as my girl-hood friend Daisy Hewlett!"

It was with difficulty that Angelina found her voice, realising that both the ladies were expecting her to speak.

"It is . . . very . . . very kind of you," she said, but the words did not sound like her own.

Then hardly above a whisper she managed to ask:

"When is . . . your party?"

"What night would you expect it to be?" Lady Hewlett said. "Tomorrow, of course!"

Angelina felt a wave of relief sweep over her and she hardly heard Lady Hewlett's voice as she continued:

"You may think it strange, Lily, that we will not be at Buckingham Palace, but I expect you have already learnt that as the King has been so ill, the invitations to the Banquet which should have taken place in June have been considerably reduced."

"No, I had not heard that," Lady Medwin replied.

"The King and Queen will now entertain only their relations, and Heaven knows there are enough of those! And of course there will be other Royalty."

"I think they are wise," Lady Medwin said, "I should have thought that after all those exhausting hours in the Abbey, it would have been sensible for the King to rest."

"He will have an hour or so to lie down between the Ceremony and the Banquet," Lady Hewlett said, "but I agree with you, it is madness to over-tax his strength after all he has been through."

"Yes, indeed," Lady Medwin agreed.

"In France they did not think he had a chance of survival," Lady Hewlett went on, "but as I said at the time, and my words have been proven true, no country in the world has better Surgeons than we have in England."

Angelina could not wait to hear any more.

She left her grandmother's room, knowing that the two old ladies would want to gossip to each other, and went up to her own bed-room.

There she sat down on the bed, feeling as if her legs could no longer carry her.

The most terrifying moments she had ever experienced had been when she thought that she might have had to let the Prince know that she could not see him tonight.

A week ago, she would have been wild with excitement at the thought of going to a party at Lady Hewlett's.

The Ambassadress had always been kind to her when she had first come to live with her grandmother, but she had been abroad for the last nine months.

Angelina knew that her parties were always filled with intelligent and important people, and she, being so young, was extremely lucky to be included amongst them.

But if in fact it had been for tonight, she knew that she would have hated every minute that she was prevented from being with the Prince.

Tomorrow was different. Tomorrow he would be at Buckingham Palace and she could go to Lady Hewlett's without feeling there might have been a chance of being with him.

Even so, she knew, because she loved him, that however glamorous the party might be, however many attractive men she might meet, it would be hard to concentrate her thoughts on anyone except the man she had met because Twi-Twi had chased the ginger cat.

Lady Hewlett stayed with her grandmother for over an hour.

When she left, Angelina escorted her down the stairs to the front door and waved as she drove away in her exceedingly smart carriage drawn by two horses.

Then she went back upstairs to her grandmother's bed-room.

Lady Medwin was looking immeasurably better because she had had a visitor.

"Daisy knows all the gossip," she said as Angelina entered the room. "I enjoyed seeing her more than I have enjoyed anything for a long time."

"I am so glad, Grandmama."

"She has some charming young men she wants to introduce to you while she is in England."

"H-how ... kind."

"It has made me see how remiss I have been in not making other arrangements for you once I became ill," Lady Medwin went on. " 'A girl should marry early,' Daisy said to me, 'and the sooner Angelina finds a husband the better!' "

Angelina started.

"A ... h-husband, Grandmama?"

"Daisy is right," Lady Medwin continued. "I married when I was just eighteen, and my mother always said that eligible bachelors get fewer as one gets older."

Angelina found this hard to puzzle out. She was hoping desperately that her grandmother would not get a fixed idea in her head that she must be married.

Lady Medwin, as her son knew, could be determined to the point of obstinacy when she wanted something.

No arguments could make her change her mind, and opposition usually strengthened her resolve to get her own way.

"I am quite happy with you, Grandmama," Angelina said quickly. "So do not let us worry about my being married for a very long time."

"That is nonsense!" Lady Medwin retorted. "And it is dear Daisy who has made me see the error of my ways."

"We will wait until you are well, then talk about it," Angelina said soothingly.

"We shall do nothing of the sort!" Lady Medwin replied. "When Daisy goes back to Paris, I shall get in touch with some of my other friends and ask them to chaperone you during the Winter Season. Oh, dear, I am really angry with myself that I did not think of doing this before!"

"Please, Grandmama, do not worry about it," Angelina begged. "I am happy, very happy here. I love reading to you and taking Twi-Twi into the garden. I have really not had time to think of parties or Balls."

She realised that her grandmother was not attending to her.

"I must buy you some new gowns, Angelina," she said. "Tell *Madame* Marguerite to call here on Monday morning, and that other dressmaker whose designs I liked—what was her name?"

"Grandmama, I have lots and lots of gowns I have not worn yet," Angelina protested.

"Just do as you are told, dearest child," her grandmother said, "and tomorrow we will make a list of my friends who I know will help me, as dearest Daisy is so willing to do."

'It is hopeless,' Angelina thought.

Now she would never be able to convince her grandmother that things were perfectly all right as they were.

And yet, she asked herself when she went to her room to change, would it not ease the agony she was going to feel when the Prince had left England if she had other things to think about than the emptiness of the Ministry next door?

But for a moment Angelina could think of nothing but the evening that lay ahead.

She would see him ... she would talk to him ... they would be together and ... She stopped her thoughts and felt herself blush as she knew how much she wanted him to kiss her again.

Perhaps it would be impossible tonight ... perhaps he would not want her ... perhaps ...

Her thoughts went round and round like a squirrel in a treadmill, but all the time an irrepressible excitement was rising in her breast and she felt as if fireworks might explode round her!

It was, she knew, simply because there was now only a very little time left before she would be with the Prince again.

She had difficulty in choosing what she thought was her second most attractive gown, because, as she had told her grandmother, there were quite a number of them in her wardrobe which she had not yet worn.

She finally put on one which was as different as possible from the one in which he had already seen her.

It was a more simple gown, of very pale blue, the colour of a thrush's egg, and was trimmed with little velvet bows of the same colour interspersed amongst flounces of shadowy lace so fine that it might have been made by fairy's fingers.

There was lace on the bodice, and when she was ready Angelina looked very young and very fragile, like a spring flower coming into bloom after the snows of winter.

At the last moment she thought that perhaps the Prince would prefer her to have worn something more formal and elaborate, but it was too late. Ruston would be waiting in the Dining-Room to serve her dinner.

She ran down the stairs, Twi-Twi following her, and when she entered the Dining-Room, Ruston said reproachfully:

"Your soup's getting cold, Miss Angelina."

This, Angelina knew, was quite impossible, considering that the silver cover was on the tureen and the soup would have been on the point of boiling when Mrs. Briggs tipped it out of the saucepan.

"I am sorry, Ruston," she said meekly.

Once again she went through the pretence of eating, slipping everything back into the dishes on the sideboard as soon as Ruston left the room. As usual, he protested because she had eaten so little.

"You're not eating enough, Miss Angelina, to keep a

mouse alive, and that's a fact!" he said with the affectionate anxiety of an old retainer.

"I am so excited about the Coronation, Ruston," Angelina replied.

She thought as she left the Dining-Room that that was definitely true.

It was her little bit of the Coronation and it was more exciting than anything else in the whole world.

She had hurried so much that when she came downstairs, wearing a chiffon wrap of the same colour over her gown and carrying Twi-Twi she realised that the hands of the clock in the Hall were only pointing to ten-past-eight.

It would be impossible for her to wait in the Mews if the Prince was not there, so Angelina waited in the doorway of the Study, from where she could see the grandfather-clock.

Twice she thought the clock itself must have stopped, because the hands moved so slowly, but at last it was only a few seconds to quarter-past and she sped down the passage towards the garden door.

She let herself out, ran across the paved garden, and opened the door into the Mews.

As she did so, she found herself facing the Prince.

She looked up into his face, her heart turned a somersault, and there was a constriction in her throat which made it impossible to speak.

She could only stand looking at him as he was looking at her. Then he spoke first.

"I have to tell you," he said in a very low voice, "that we are not going to the party alone."

"N-not . . . alone?" Angelina repeated.

"There was such a fuss because they believed I was out alone last night," the Prince said, "that I had to agree to take one of my Aides-de-Camp with me."

He must have seen the disappointment in Angelina's face, for he said:

117

"You know, my darling, that I long to be alone with you. I want it more than I can possibly say, but I have to do what the Minister and all the rest of them want."

"Would you ... rather I did not ... come?"

It was difficult to say the words because they seemed to stick on her tongue, but somehow she managed it.

"No, of course not," the Prince replied. "You have to come. You must come! Leave everything to me. I will manage somehow so that I can talk to you alone."

He saw her eyes light up and he said, still in a voice so low that it could not be overheard:

"I have been waiting for this moment all day. It has been unmitigated hell to know you were so near and yet I could not see you."

"I ... waited in the ... garden."

"Do you suppose I was not aware of that?" the Prince asked, and his voice was raw. "I thought of you and I longed to be with you, but it was impossible."

"I ... I knew that."

Now he was there, she was near to him, and it was almost as if they were one person as they had been last night.

"I love you!" the Prince said. "I would have thought it impossible, but you look even more beautiful than you did last night."

He smiled and suddenly everything was changed as he said in a very different tone of voice:

"Come, let us go to the party and forget all our problems, at least for the next few hours."

He drew Angelina towards the carriage, and as they reached it a young man hastily stepped out.

He would have been considered handsome, she thought, if one had not instantly compared him with the Prince.

"May I present," the Prince asked, "Captain Aristotelis Soutsos, who is not only my Aide-de-Camp but a very old friend since we went to School together."

Angelina held out her hand and Captain Soutsos bowed over it.

They got into the carriage and the Aide-de-Camp sat on the small seat and Angelina put Twi-Twi beside him.

"Will he bite me?" Captain Soutsos asked.

"He might," Angelina replied, "so I advise you not to touch him. He does not really like being touched by strangers."

"He has never tried to bite me," the Prince said.

"Perhaps he did not think you were a stranger," Angelina said, without thinking.

Then, as she met the Prince's eyes, she knew that they were both aware that in fact they had never been strangers.

From the first moment there had been that awareness that their feelings for each other were unique.

"Aristotelis and I have had a most exhausting day," the Prince said. "It started immediately after breakfast, with meetings at which everyone said too much and nobody listened."

Captain Soutsos laughed.

"That is very true, Sir."

"You will find," the Prince said, addressing Angelina, "that the Greeks can be very verbose when they get onto a subject about which they feel deeply."

"Were those the sort of subjects you were discussing today, Sir?" Angelina asked.

"I certainly felt deeply about most of them," the Prince replied, "if nobody else did."

He spoke in a manner which told Angelina, without his having to explain, that they had been discussing his marriage.

Because she wanted him to be happy when they were together, she changed the subject and told him how her grandmother had been visited by Lady Hewlett, and how she was to dine with her and the Ambassador at a party the next evening.

119

"I know His Excellency," the Prince said. "He is a very intelligent man. I only wish the Ambassadors whom Britain sends to Greece had half his understanding and tact."

"You sound as if you were dissatisfied with our representatives," Angelina said half-jokingly.

"Not exactly dissatisfied," the Prince said. "I just wish they had a little more knowledge of the country in which they fly the British flag."

Captain Soutsos laughed.

"You are making me think of the Lord High Commissioners of the Ionian Islands when they came under British protection after the Napoleonic War."

The Prince laughed too and Angelina asked:

"Were they extraordinary?"

"They were certainly great individualists, or shall I say eccentrics, to put it mildly," the Prince replied. "They were very important and made certain the Greeks were well aware of it."

"The first Commissioner," Captain Soutsos interposed, "Sir Thomas Maitland, was notorious for his rudeness, especially to anyone bearing a letter of introduction."

"The next was certainly no better," the Prince interrupted, as if he wished himself to tell the story to Angelina. "Sir Frederick Adam married an ambitious Corfiote whose moustache, according to contemporary cartoons and biographies, would not have shamed a dashing Hussar!"

"I do not believe it!" Angelina said with a laugh.

"It is true, unless the history-books lie!" the Prince averred. "And this peculiarity did not prevent the Commissioner from lavishing most of the revenue of the islands on the hairy lady!"

"Let us be fair," Captain Soutsos objected. "Successive British Commissioners did build roads, hospitals, asylums, and prisons."

"For the latter, of course, their conquered people

were extremely grateful!" the Prince said, his eyes twinkling.

All the way to their destination Captain Soutsos vied with the Prince in telling Angelina amusing incidents which had happened in the long-distant past.

Because they made her laugh, because the Prince seemed almost boyish when he was indulging in a verbal duel with his Aide-de-Camp, she thought the evening, despite the fact that she was not alone with the Prince, would be a happy one.

She was not mistaken.

When they arrived at what appeared to be a rather small and unimportant Greek Restaurant off Shaftesbury Avenue, an excited little band of Cephalonians rushed out to greet them.

They entered a large, low-ceilinged room and Angelina found that there were over a hundred people waiting for them, who clapped when they appeared.

The whole place was decorated, not with flags and bunting like the streets, but with garlands of flowers and leaves made into intricate designs that Angelina was sure had been the work of the Greek girls.

There were a number of them present, all, she thought, very beautiful, with their huge, dark, long-lashed eyes and their hair braided round their heads in thick plaits.

They wore their national dress, and she knew that nothing could be more becoming than the large white handkerchief or head-scarf with one end flung over the left shoulder and the other hanging to the waist, a scarlet bodice faced with yellow, full white sleeves, a long dark blue skirt, and a pale blue apron with diagonal yellow stripes.

It made the Restaurant seem vivid with colour, and the Prince and Angelina were led to a table at the far end which was decorated with flowers. The rest of the guests sat at long tables drawn close to the walls, leaving the centre of the room free.

Angelina knew that this was for the dancing which would come later, but now she looked curiously at the dishes that were put in front of them.

The Prince accepted an aperitif of *Ouze*, a spirit he told Angelina, with the flavour of aniseed, which she would not like.

She was conscious, as he spoke, that while they were talking in words to which anyone could listen, they were saying things to each other which could not be heard but which linked them together with the mesmeric magic they had known the night before.

"You are looking very beautiful," the Prince whispered almost under his breath.

The light in her eyes answered him, and in a normal voice he said:

"You must try *Mezé*, which I know you will enjoy."

A big plate of *Mezé* was put in front of them and the Prince helped Angelina to a small canapé spread with *brik*, which he told her was red caviar, and *taramosaláta*, which she found was a delicious preparation of fish roes.

There were cucumbers, yoghurt, garlic, and olives of various sorts, green and black, and the Prince told her that a Greek could recognise from which part of Greece each came.

She looked at them in surprise, thinking they all looked the same.

"The oval olive," he explained, "comes from Delphi, and the pointed one from Kalamata."

Angelina took an oval olive and they smiled at each other, knowing that at Delphia was the Temple of Apollo.

Afterwards it was difficult for her to remember all the different dishes she sampled, but they were all delicious.

There was fish prepared with a special sauce of oil and lemon-juice, and there was *souvlákia*, which were kabobs of meat on a skewer roasted on charcoal, which the Prince told her was a favourite dish in Greece.

There were *Dolmádes*, which were vine-leaves folded round mince and rice, and Angelina really felt that she could eat no more by the time the desserts were brought to the table.

But she could not resist *Baklavà*, a sticky sweet-meat made of honey and nuts covered with a flaky pastry, and the Prince would not allow her to refuse a handleless cup of Turkish coffee.

"It is called *Skéto* without sugar and *Méthio* with it," he said.

Angelina laughed.

"I really did know that. I have been trying to study Greek all by myself, but the difficulty is that although I know how a great number of words are spelt, I cannot pronounce them."

"I will teach you the ones that are important," he said caressingly.

Then even as he spoke, they both realised that there would be no time to do so.

"Perhaps," Angelina said, "your Minister will be ... able to recommend a Greek ... teacher."

As she spoke, she thought it a possibility, and she was not prepared for the sudden anger which flashed into the Prince's face.

"Do you think I want anyone except myself to teach you anything?" he asked.

When, because of his tone of voice, she looked at him in surprise, she saw the pain in his eyes and was once again aware of how desperately he was suffering.

When dinner was finished the dancing began, and now Angelina saw, as she had always wanted to, the traditional Greek dances, which were referred to in almost every book she read but which were difficult to visualise unless one actually saw them.

The Orchestra was certainly a strange one, but she soon realised that there were particular instruments for certain dances.

The first dance was only for the men, and although they looked large and heavy and many of them, Angelina thought, were porters in the market or wagon-drivers, they danced with a panther-like grace.

Linked by a coloured handkerchief in each hand, they bounded to and fro with a swirling motion which gave the impression of the bindings of a chain.

"This is symbolic," the Prince explained, "of a people sticking together in adversity and supporting one another."

The women joined in for a dance performed in a circle while a male leader waved a handkerchief, swirling, pointing, and lunging as if brandishing a sword with a remarkably acrobatic skill.

While he did so, a chain of dancers shuffled round, their arms entwined, and they were accompanied by a lyre, drums, a clarinet, and a very scratchy violin.

The Greek dances went on for a long time, and while the Prince refused to take part because he did not wish to leave Angelina, Captain Soutsos was dancing as energetically as the rest.

Angelina noticed that he was smiling at a very pretty young girl who seemed, however much the dancers twisted and turned, always to be at his side.

She was watching wide-eyed when the Prince said quietly in her ear:

"Shall we go?"

"Can we?" Angelina asked.

As the music came to an end, the Prince rose to his feet.

He made a short speech in Greek, and because he spoke so clearly, Angelina understood quite a lot of what he said.

He thanked the Cephalonians for inviting him and

told them how much he appreciated their loyalty and their continued love of their country.

He said that he would take home with him the conviction that Cephalonians would always be the same, wherever they might find themselves, and that they would never lose their initiative, their courage, and their patriotism.

The Prince's speech was hailed with cries of "Bravo!" And then with Angelina beside him, they walked down the centre of the room, and the guests, with their hands held above their heads, clapped them all the way to the door.

Only as they reached it and Captain Soutsos joined them did the Prince say:

"You stay, Aristotelis. As far as you are concerned, the night is still young and there are many other places in London where you will enjoy yourself."

"You are quite certain, Sir, that I should not accompany you home?" the Aide-de-Camp asked.

"I assure you that in the morning I will cover up any of your deficiencies in that respect," the Prince replied.

Captain Soutsos stole a quick glance at Angelina and she knew that he realised that the Prince did not want him with them any more than he wished to return to the Ministry.

"Thank you, Sir," he said. "Good-night, Miss Medwin."

"Good-night, Captain," Angelina replied.

They stepped into the carriage, and after Twi-Twi had joined them from the box where he had been sitting beside Alexis, they drove off.

The Prince waited until they were out of sight of the Restaurant, then put his arm about Angelina and drew her against him.

"At last!" he said. "I thought we should never have a chance of being alone."

Her heart had started beating frantically, and at the

first touch of his arm she felt the lightning flash through her and an overwhelming excitement rising in her throat.

"I love you!" the Prince said. "I can think of nothing else to say except that I love you!"

"It has . . . been a very . . . long day," Angelina whispered.

"I know, I know," he said. "It was an unbelievable agony to sit in the Council Chamber listening to Costas drooling on about his troubles and the Prime Minister wanting to talk of nothing but my marriage."

Angelina did not speak and the Prince went on as if he felt that she must know what had been happening.

"There was a letter from my Cousin Theodoros today. He says that he has something of very great importance to tell me—something which concerns the revolutionary element in the South of the island."

"What do you think it is?" Angelina asked.

"I have no idea," the Prince answered, "but it means, my precious, that I shall have to return to Cephalonia as soon as the Coronation is over."

"Oh . . . no . . . no!"

She knew, even as he spoke, that this was what she had anticipated. He would have to leave, and she might never see him again.

"What can I do?" the Prince asked. "I can hardly write and say that I am no longer vitally concerned with the trouble in Cephalonia, because I am in love."

He pulled her close against him as he spoke, and looked down into her face to say:

"Yet you know that that is true."

She could see him quite clearly by the light from the gas-lamps, and the illumination swept away so much of the darkness that even the inside of their closed carriage seemed filled with light.

"I love you too," Angelina said, "but I know that you have to do your duty to your country, and we . . . have to be . . . brave."

"My sweet! My precious!" the Prince cried. "Was there ever anyone like you?"

His last words were lost against her lips as his mouth took possession of hers.

He kissed her until once again he swept her up into the sky and she could think of nothing but the wonder and glory that surrounded them.

She knew that this was what she had been praying for and yearning for all day and all night, but she had been afraid at the back of her mind that nothing could ever be quite so wonderful and so ecstatic as their kiss in St. James's Park.

But now she felt new emotions awakening within her, sensations that she did not even know existed.

Their love seemed to grow and expand until it carried them ever higher and higher into the sky.

The Prince must have instructed Alexis before they left the Mews not to carry them home too quickly, and when Angelina came back to earth, she realised that they were in darkness as they were no longer passing through the streets.

Instead they were driving through Hyde Park, travelling, she thought, the long way round.

"I cannot leave you," the Prince said.

Then with a deep sigh he asked:

"Why could I not have fallen in love with someone I should be allowed to marry? Or else with someone I could have taken back with me to Cephalonia and kept secretly near the Palace, so that whenever I was free we could be together?"

Angelina was still for a moment, then she said in a very small voice:

"Are you . . . asking me . . . to do . . . that?"

"No!" the Prince said positively. "I told you, my precious one, that I would never hurt you, and neither would I insult you or our love by suggesting such a thing."

127

He made a little sound that was half a groan and
half a cry of despair.

"I am only saying that there are barriers round you
which I cannot cross, and even if I could, I would
want to leave you as you are, pure and untouched; my
Persephone, who belongs to me with her heart, her
soul, and her mind."

That was true, Angelina thought, and she understood exactly what he was trying to say to her. But she
knew, as he did, that there was no solution.

She could not help thinking, however, that it would
be very wonderful to be with him even as his mistress.

Then she knew that if she agreed to such an idea, it
would soil the perfection of their love and the sanctity
which underlay their kiss and their feelings towards
each other.

"Perhaps," she said hesitatingly after a moment, "if
... if we cannot ... be together in this life ... there
will be ... others."

"Is that enough for you or for me?" the Prince asked.
"I want you now! I want you so violently, so uncon-
trollably, Angelina, that after I take you home tonight
I can never see you again."

Angelina gave a little cry.

"Do-do you ... mean that?"

"I knew last night when I let you go without kissing
you again," he said, "that I had reached the breaking-
point."

There was a raw agony in his voice that made her
slip her fingers into his and hold on to him tightly.

"I am not an Englishman," the Prince said. "I am a
Greek and my love is something greater than myself
—greater than my pride and perhaps even my hon-
our."

His voice deepened as he went on:

"I want you, Angelina! I want you not only as a
goddess in a shrine at which I worship, but as a woman. I want you to belong to me not only with your

mind, as you already do, but with your lovely, exqui-site body."

He spoke with a violence which made Angelina think that if she did not love him so overwhelmingly, she might have been afraid of him.

Instead, she only pressed herself a little closer to him and tightened her fingers on his.

"Even if I had not had the letter from my cousin urging me to return immediately," the Prince said, "I should have gone the day after tomorrow."

Angelina felt her lips were too stiff and dry to re-ply, but somehow she managed to say:

"I . . . I understand."

"Do you?" the Prince asked. "No—it is impossible! You are too pure and innocent, Angelina, to know that I am being tempted by all the devils in hell to take you while I have the opportunity!"

There was silence before he went on in a quieter tone:

"But between us there stands an angel with a flam-ing sword—your angel, my darling, who is protecting you, even if you are unaware of it, from a man who is burning in the unquenchable fire of hell."

He raised her hand to his lips as he spoke and kissed it passionately, possessively, and she knew that as he was determined to control himself, he dared not kiss her lips.

The carriage had come to a standstill beside the bridge of the Serpentine. The Prince looked out through the open window and Angelina could see the water glimmering silver beneath the moon and the stars.

"I thought before we set out tonight," he said hoarsely, "that I could walk with you under the trees to where we sat that first magical afternoon when I told you about myself and you tried to help me."

He kissed her hand again before he said:

"But instead, you made me fall so deeply and wildly in love with you that I know I never will love another woman."

"I want you to be . . . happy," Angelina said.

"That will be impossible," the Prince replied, "since I cannot live with you, and, loving you as I do, I dare not go with you now out into the moonlight."

"I . . . want to be with you . . . beside the . . . water," Angelina whispered.

"Do not tempt me," the Prince cried almost roughly. "I have already said, Angelina, that I am weak, and if I touch you, if I hold you close to me and there is nothing to restrain me—I may do something we should both of us regret afterwards."

There was a look in his eyes and an expression on his face which she had never seen before. By the light of the moon, which came in faintly through the carriage window, she thought for a moment that he looked sinister.

Then she knew that whatever he did, whatever he said, however uncontrolled he might be, she still loved him.

But she understood even better than he did that their love must not be spoilt.

With an effort that seemed almost to tear her apart, she said in a low voice:

"Let us go . . . back."

The Prince bent forward and knocked on the wall of the carriage above Twi-Twi's head.

The horse moved forward and crossed over the Serpentine, and as they drove into the light from the gas-lamps, Angelina could see that the Prince's expression was grim and stern.

He looked immeasurably older and she thought the lines on his face were sharply etched because they were lines of pain.

They drove in silence, and yet she was tinglingly aware that their hands were touching and that he held her close against him.

They were driving back through the lighted streets, and yet Angelina felt as if they had stepped from the light into a darkness which would encompass them both for the rest of their lives.

"Will you watch me going to the Abbey tomorrow?" the Prince asked at length. "I would rather you did not."

"I ... m-must see ... you," Angelina said. "And you ... promised me my ... little bit of the ... Coronation."

"To me it might as well be a funeral pyre," the Prince said savagely.

Angelina drew in her breath.

"Please," she said, "will you ... listen to me ... for a moment?"

"You know I will listen to your voice as I always shall whenever I am alone," the Prince replied.

"Then ... you must not ... fight against the ... impossible," Angelina said. "It will ... only harm you ... like hitting your ... head against a brick wall. We have to accept that ... this is ... f-fate ... and there is nothing we can ... do about it."

"You are very wise, my darling," he said, "but I cannot control my own feelings."

"You are controlling them," Angelina replied very softly.

He turned to look at her for the first time since they had left the Serpentine, and now he said, in a very different tone of voice:

"I love you—I admire you—I worship you! Everything about you is perfect—so absolutely right. You are not only saying the right thing—but you are thinking it. It is there in the light which always envelops you, the light from which I can never escape until my dying day."

"Do you ... want to?" Angelina asked. "Are you ... sorry we ... met each other?"

"Sorry?" the Prince cried. "It is the most wonderful

131

thing that has ever come into my life, and I know, Angelina, that even when you are not there, you will inspire me to do what is right."

He made a gesture with his hands, as if he knew that there was no point in stating the obvious.

"The legends of Greece are usually tragic and end unhappily," he said. "We are part of our own legend, but because of you, and this is true, Angelina, I shall try to be a better Ruler and a better man than I have been in the past."

"Do ... you mean ... that?"

"I mean it because it is true," he answered, "and you are right—we shall meet again because what we feel for each other is greater than the confines of the body, greater than death."

Angelina felt the tears come into her eyes, and as the carriage entered Belgrave Square, the Prince turned her face up to his.

"Good-bye, my dearest, my most perfect and only love!" he said. "You will always be with me and I with you. Perhaps one day we shall find each other again."

He kissed her as he spoke, but very differently from the way in which he had kissed her before.

It was the kiss of a man who pledges himself to an ideal which is so sacred that it evokes no other emotion within him.

The carriage came to a standstill and Angelina knew that this was the end.

There was nothing more to say, nothing that could alter their future.

The Prince stepped out of the carriage and opened the garden door.

For a moment they looked at each other and she thought there was an infinite sadness in his expression which she had never seen before.

Then without speaking she moved into the garden and heard the door shut behind her.

# Chapter Six

"It's a nice morning, Miss Angelina, just as I told you it'd be," Emily said as she pulled back the curtains.

Angelina lay with her eyes still shut and did not move.

She did not wish to face the world. She only wanted to stay asleep, to forget that she had to wake up to the loneliness and the misery of knowing that she would never be with the Prince again.

Last night, when she had got into bed, she had cried until she was exhausted and her pillow was wet with tears.

Then she had forced herself to dream back into the moments of wonder when he had kissed her, when it had been impossible to think of anything but the closeness of him.

But she could not shut out from her mind or from her soul the passionate violence in his voice when he had said he wanted her to belong to him, or the knowledge within herself that it was what she wanted too.

They were one and she knew that neither of them would ever be complete without the other. But tomorrow he would go back to Cephalonia and she would be left in England: there would be half of

Europe lying between them and a loneliness that was beyond expression.

She could not help feeling that if she were the one to be in Greece it would have been easier to bear.

There would be the light, the feeling of being close to the gods, and the inescapable knowledge that all things pass.

Then she told herself that wherever either of them were it would still be the same. They needed each other and she believed the Prince when he said she inspired him.

It was not just she herself alone who brought that about; it was love that was greater than either of them; love which came from God and was so divine that it made the Prince treat her as something sacred.

But because he was a man, and a very masculine and virile man, he desired her as a woman.

"Now what'll you be wearing today, Miss Angelina?" Emily asked, breaking in on her thoughts.

Angelina wanted to reply that all she wished for was "sack-cloth and ashes," but she knew that Emily would not understand and would be shocked by such a remark.

Although she longed to tell the old housemaid to go away and leave her alone, she knew that that would be unkind.

She remembered too that if she did not wish to get up and face the world, Twi-Twi, who had jumped down from her bed as soon as Emily opened the door, would want to go out.

He expected her life to revolve round him with a punctuality which made him resent it if she was ever late.

"Which gown do you think I ought to wear, Emily?" Angelina asked, though she had no interest in what to choose.

Yesterday she had chosen what she thought was her prettiest day-dress because she had hoped the Prince might see her, and last night she had known by the look in his eyes that she had chosen the right gown to go with him to the Cephalonian Restaurant.

Today there would be only the servants to notice if she was wearing a pretty dress or her night-gown.

It came to her mind almost with a feeling of horror that this evening she would have to dress up to dine with Lord and Lady Hewlett.

How could she make herself pleasant to the man who would sit on either side of her, and to those who later would ask her to dance, when all she longed for was to be in the Prince's arms?

She knew she would automatically do what was required of her, but while she went through all the motions, she would in reality be dead, because the light of the spirit would have gone from her.

That was what the Prince was taking away with him, back to Cephalonia, the light which the Greeks had seen in those they loved, the light which the Prince had said had enveloped her when she had turned round to face him in the Hall at the Ministry.

It was the light, Angelina thought, that as far as she was concerned would never shine again.

When she was dressed, putting on without looking at it the dress that Emily had laid ready for her on the chair, she went down to breakfast.

Only when Ruston kept saying what a splendid day it was for the new King, and how everyone would rejoice that he was well enough to be crowned, did she realise that she had on a very elaborate gown that her grandmother had bought for her to wear at a garden-party.

It was of lace and chiffon and made Angelina think, when she had first seen it, that she looked like a fairy Princess. But now, elaborate and beautiful though it was, she felt like a peasant and a pauper.

"Without love I have nothing!" she told herself.

She went up to say good-morning to her grand-

mother, then took Twi-Twi to the garden for his first
and shortest walk.

She knew the Prince had said he would not see her
again, and yet, irrepressibly, she felt tense and excited just in case he should change his mind.

The sunshine was golden on the trees and the flowers, but the minutes dragged by one after another until
it was time for her to go back to the house.

Unreasonably disappointed, she knew that whatever
the Prince might say, she was determined to see him
when she came out later.

He would be leaving for the Abbey at eleven o'clock
and she calculated at what time he would be return-
ing after the long Service.

The rest of the Ministry, who were not to be in the
procession to Buckingham Palace, would return by a
quicker route and would therefore be waiting to re-
ceive him.

Then, Angelina thought, there could be several hours
when they might meet each other before the Prince
left again for the Banquet, which was to take place in
the evening.

She suddenly felt frantically that she could not bear
it, that she must speak to him just once more, must tell
him again of her love.

He had forbidden it and she felt like crying out that
he did not really love her! Otherwise how could he let
those precious moments pass when they might be together?

Then she told herself it was because his love was so
great, so overwhelming, that he had been strong
enough last night to refuse to walk by the Serpentine
because he might have upset or shocked her.

No man, she thought, could have made a bigger personal sacrifice, and it would be wrong for her to try
and tempt him from the course on which he had set
himself.

"I love you!" she whispered as she left the garden,

hoping, as she had hoped before, that her thoughts would reach him in the Ministry and he would know she was thinking of him.

There were all the usual things to do, just as she had done them for months.

She read the newspapers to her grandmother and even managed to remain apparently unmoved when Lady Medwin wondered curiously why the Prince's name did not appear in any list of guests at the parties and Receptions which had taken place the previous night.

"Perhaps he is secretly courting some Princess," she remarked.

"Why should you think ... that, Grandmama?" Angelina asked.

"Daisy Hewlett told me that he is here to find a wife. There are quite a number of eligible Princesses about, so he should have no difficulty."

Angelina did not answer. The agony she had felt before, when she thought of the Prince being married, had now just become a dull ache that seemed to have spread over her whole body.

"You look a little pale this morning," Lady Medwin exclaimed suddenly, making her jump. "You had better go out in the sunshine and see if it will put some colour into your cheeks."

"I would like to do that, Grandmama."

"The King has certainly got a fine day for his Coronation," Lady Medwin said, "but I hope the whole long palaver of being crowned does not send him back to bed. If you ask my opinion, it is far too soon for him to be doing anything so strenuous."

They talked about the King for a short while, until at last Angelina could escape and run downstairs with a little more liveliness than she had done earlier, because now she would be able to see the Prince and watch him set off for the Abbey.

As usual, there was no-one in the garden, and she

137

set Twi-Twi down before she pushed her way through the bushes to her usual secret place, from which she could watch the Ministry.

The lilacs and laurels had grown very thick during the summer and it was quite a struggle to get through them, but finally Angelina could face the front door of the Ministry and could see without being seen.

Already the red carpet was in position, but the front door was shut and she waited for quite some minutes before there was the sound of a carriage coming along the Square.

She saw that, drawn by two horses, it was closed, and she realised that the Minister and the other officials who would be in the Abbey had not yet left.

The carriage drew up outside the front door.

Now a number of flunkeys in their colourful livery came hurrying out, and a minute later the first carriage was joined by another, also closed.

Angelina watched with interest.

She saw the Minister come out first and she recognised him because she had seen him on several occasions before.

He was followed by another man who, she knew, was a high-ranking official, though she was not quite certain what was his position, then two others.

They all got into the first carriage and drove off, and the next one moved into place.

Now there was a dark, bearded man who seemed of some importance and wore a magnificent and very impressive gold-embroidered uniform.

Angelina was certain that he was Kharilaos Costas, the Foreign Minister, and he was accompanied by three other officials.

The carriage drove away, and now from the direction of the Mews, Angelina recognised Alexis driving an open carriage drawn by four horses.

There was a footman on the box beside him and another standing up behind, and as they drew up outside the Ministry Angelina found herself holding her breath, because at any moment she would see the Prince again.

He came out onto the steps and her heart seemed to do a double somersault and she felt that she wanted to cry out and tell him how magnificent he looked.

His uniform had a number of decorations which glinted in the sunshine, but she found it impossible to look at anything but his handsome face, and she saw that his expression was stern and unsmiling.

As he stood on the top of the steps, he looked for a moment towards the garden and she knew he was thinking of her.

'I love you! Oh, my darling, I love you!' she cried in her heart.

His expression did not alter, and she felt, sadly, that he had not received her message.

He stepped into the carriage, sitting alone on the back seat, while Captain Soutsos, very smart in his uniform, sat with another Aide-de-Camp opposite him.

The Ministry footmen bowed as the carriage drove away and Angelina watched until it turned the corner of the Square and was out of sight.

"I shall see him just once more," she told herself dismally, "then that will be the end!"

She went to the seat where they had first sat together near the geranium-filled flower-bed and thought of how they had talked so casually to each other and how, even then, she had felt as if she vibrated to everything he said.

It was as if a strange, irresistible force drew them together so that she could never escape from him.

She sat there for a long time, thinking, then slowly she walked back to the house, knowing she had only one thing left to look forward to—the Prince's return.

Angelina had expected her grandmother to have her usual sleep in the afternoon, but when she went up to see her after luncheon Lady Medwin had other ideas.

"It is too boring to sleep when I might have been in Westminster Abbey, seeing the Coronation for myself," she said. "What I suggest we do, dearest child, is that you read to me about Queen Victoria's Coronation. It is in a book in the Study. See if you can find it. Then we can both feel we are in the Abbey."

Angelina found the book without much difficulty and went upstairs again to her grandmother's bedroom.

As she read in her low, sweet voice, her thoughts kept wandering to the Prince, seeing the colourful ceremony taking place and surrounded by all the other Royalty like himself.

However, the newspapers reported sadly that it was not to have the same glory and magnificence which would have been there in June.

Then the trains had rolled into Victoria Station almost every half hour, bearing Royal visitors who had come from all over the world.

Angelina had then read out the full list of guests, which had seemed like the pages in a fairy-tale.

She remembered how romantic His Imperial Highness the Hereditary Grand Duke Michael of Russia had sounded, and His Serene Highness the Hereditary Prince of Morocco.

She had stumbled over the pronunciation of the names of His Imperial Highness the Yi Chai-Kak, the Prince of Evi-Yang, Ras Makunan of Ethiopia, and Said Ali of Zanzibar.

But today a great number of the strange names and titles were not there. It had been too much to make the long journey twice.

But Lady Medwin laughed when they were told by *The Times* that the Abyssinian Special Mission were present for the simple reason that they had never dared to go home.

"*They would have lost face,*" the newspaper explained, *"if they had returned to Abyssinia without having seen the crowning of the great white Potentate!"*

Lady Medwin, who had not wasted her time with Lady Hewlett, had little pieces of information of her own to impart.

"Daisy said," she announced, "that the octogenarian Archbishop of Canterbury is looking so feeble that everybody is saying he will never survive the ceremony."

"How awful if the poor old man should die while he is actually crowning the King!" Angelina said.

"It would certainly be a catastrophe," Lady Medwin agreed, "and we must just pray that such a disaster does not happen."

Angelina remembered the Prince saying that incidents that happened in the Abbey were only amusing if one had someone with whom to share them.

She wondered if tonight he would wish he could share with her anything that had amused him.

'I love you! I love you!' she was crying in her heart, until with a sense of relief she realised that it was time to take Twi-Twi to the garden.

Unfortunately, Lady Medwin was in one of her chattering moods.

She kept Angelina talking about one thing and another until she felt frantic in case the Prince should return and she would not be there to see him.

"Twi-Twi wants to go out, Grandmama," she said at length, giving the Pekingese a little push with her foot.

He was sleeping quite peacefully on the carpet and snorted indignantly at being treated in such a manner, but Lady Medwin said at once:

"Then you had better go, dearest, but do not be too long. I have a lot of things to talk to you about and I really feel better today. It must be because there is so much excitement in the air."

"I will not be long, Grandmama," Angelina promised.

She thought, as she spoke, that once the Prince had gone inside the Ministry there would be no point in staying in the garden.

She went down the stairs, picked up her hat, which she had left in the Hall as usual, and put it on.

Ruston handed her the key and she crossed the road and let herself into the garden.

Before she did so she looked at the Ministry and saw that the red carpet was down and there were several flunkeys standing at the top of the steps.

She guessed that the Prime Minister and the other Statesmen would have already returned and now there was only the Prince to arrive. Doubtless he would have to join them in yet another of the long conferences which he found so boring.

'They will talk to him about his marriage,' Angelina thought.

She knew how much he would hate the continual discussions over a subject which was now even more painful than it had been before he had met her.

There was no doubt that he would have to marry.

Even Lady Hewlett was expecting him to take a wife, which showed that his choice was being discussed in Paris and doubtless in the other Embassies and Ministries all over Europe.

Once again, Angelina thought, the day would come when she would read of his wedding, and she knew that it would be a sword-thrust in her heart, inflicting a wound that could never heal.

She locked the garden gate behind her, then moved towards the bushes where she had concealed herself this morning.

As she did so, she had the idea that she might watch the Prince's carriage coming along the other side of the Square first.

It would give her a chance to see more of him, and if she hurried she could run across the lawn and be back in her usual place outside the Ministry door by the time he arrived.

As if he knew exactly where he was going, Twi-Twi walked towards the clump of lilac-bushes where she had been this morning.

Angelina, however, walked past them.

She had proceeded quite a little way across the lawn before she looked back to see if Twi-Twi was following her.

'He is a creature of habit,' she thought to herself, 'and he will think it strange if there is any change.'

For a moment she could not see Twi-Twi, but then she heard him bark and it flashed through her mind that he might have had a glimpse of the Ministry cat.

She turned round, ready to go back and fetch him, then she saw that Twi-Twi was not running as he would have been if the cat were in sight, but standing outside the bushes, barking.

'I wonder what can be upsetting him,' she thought.

Then, pushing his way through the lilacs and the laurels as she had done so often, came a man.

She could not see him clearly, but he was hatless and wearing what appeared to be a black mackintosh.

As he was free of the bushes Twi-Twi barked at him again, and, to Angelina's horror, the man's right foot shot out and kicked the Pekingese, rolling him over on the grass.

She hurried forward, furious at what she had seen happen, but even as she reached Twi-Twi the man walked swiftly towards the gate, let himself out, and vanished into the road.

She picked up the small dog in her arms and hugged him.

He was growling in his throat and shaking with anger at what had occurred.

"Poor darling! How dare he do such a thing!" Angelina said soothingly, holding him close against her.

He was slightly appeased by the fuss she was making of him but she knew that his dignity had been upset and he would not forget in a hurry how badly he had been treated.

There was no time now, she thought, to go to the far side of the garden as she had intended. She had much better go to her usual place and take Twi-Twi with her.

She parted the leaves of the lilac-bushes gently so as not to frighten the Pekingese, and she was just stepping forward when suddenly she saw something which made her stand very still.

There was already somebody in her usual place of vantage.

She could see the back of a man's head through the leaves.

For a moment she felt affronted that anyone should take what was her special look-out. Then she remembered that she did not own the garden and that every other householder in the Square had the right to it.

Obviously someone besides herself wanted to watch the Prince's return from the Coronation.

'I shall have to find somewhere else,' Angelina thought.

Then even as she was wondering where she should go, the man in front of her moved and she saw something shine.

For a moment it seemed so incredible that she thought she was dreaming, but then she realised that the man watching the front door of the Ministry held a rifle in his hand.

It seemed so impossible that Angelina took another long look to make quite certain.

Then she drew in her breath.

Very gently, so as not to make a noise, she backed away from the bushes where she had parted the leaves.

Standing again in the sunshine, with Twi-Twi in her arms, she thought frantically what she should do.

Her first impulse was to run to the Ministry to warn them of the danger.

Then she told herself that if she did so, the assailant would know he had been discovered and would disappear.

'He will simply try again later,' she thought, and at that moment she knew what to do.

She ran across the lawn, with Twi-Twi snorting indignantly against her breast, to the opposite gate.

She let herself out, then started to run down the road as swiftly as she could towards Grosvenor Crescent.

She knew that was the way that the Prince would return, and she could only pray that she would not be too late.

She was terrified that by the time she reached the corner of the Square the carriage might have already passed and be proceeding towards the Ministry.

But there was no sign of it and Angelina thankfully crossed the road and walked a little way up Grosvenor Crescent.

Ahead she could see the traffic at Hyde Park Corner: carriages, waggons, and horse-drawn omnibuses, all filled with people.

She knew there would be huge crowds down the Mall and clustered outside Buckingham Palace, having waited all night to cheer the King who, at last, after so much delay and anxiety, was now actually crowned.

But Angelina could think of nothing but the Prince.

His life was in danger; the revolutionaries of whom he had spoken had not waited for him to return to his own country, but were prepared to kill him here in England!

She stood on the pavement, waiting, her eyes fixed on the traffic at the end of the road.

Twi-Twi struggled in her arms.

He was hot, still very indignant at having been kicked, and did not like being held for any length of time.

Angelina, however, merely tightened her hold on him.

"You have to wait! We have to save him, Twi-Twi," she said.

Even as she spoke, she saw the horses coming towards her, and ran into the road.

She held Twi-Twi under her left arm and waved frantically with her right.

For one terrifying moment she thought that Alexis was unable to stop the horses and they would run her down. Then, within only a few feet of her, he managed to draw them to a standstill.

When she knew they would not drive on, she ran to the side of the carriage.

As she did so, the Prince bent forward to see what was happening.

She saw the expression of surprise on his face, and when she reached the side of the carriage, she found for one moment that it was impossible to speak, for her voice had gone.

"What is the . . . ?" the Prince began, but she interrupted him.

"There . . is a . . . man! A . . . man . . . waiting to . . . shoot you . . . he is . . . h-hidden with a rifle in the . . . bushes opposite the door of the . . . Ministry!"

Just for a second there was an incredulous look on the Prince's face, as if he did not believe her.

Then Captain Soutsos said:

"I will see to it, Sir."

The footman jumped down from behind to open the door of the carriage and Captain Soutsos got out, followed by the other Aide-de-Camp.

Angelina held out the key to the garden.

"If you go in by... the gate on this side," she said, "he will not see you."

"That is a good idea," Captain Soutsos said. "Thank you, Miss Medwin."

The Prince put out his hand and said:

"Come with me."

Angelina climbed into the carriage and sat beside him.

Captain Soutsos looked up at Alexis.

"Turn in at the first turning on the right and wait there until we fetch you."

Alexis raised his whip to the brim of his hat to show that he understood, and as the two Aides-de-Camp walked off, the carriage moved down Grosvenor Crescent and turned right.

There was a small garden in a crescent of tall houses and Alexis drew the carriage up in the shadow of a tree.

Angelina sat back, Twi-Twi still in her arms, feeling that she was unable to say any more, unable for the moment even to think.

She had saved the Prince, that was all that mattered, but the agony she had suffered thinking that she might not be in time to save him had left her so weak that she felt almost as if she would faint.

As if he understood what she was feeling, he took Twi-Twi from her and put him down on the opposite seat.

Then he held her hand in both of his and said quietly:

"Thank you, my darling. How could I have imagined, how could I have dreamt, that such dramatic things could happen here in the safety of England?"

Angelina felt herself quiver at the touch of his fingers, and, as if he gave her life itself, she felt her weakness disappearing and her whole body invaded as if by a stream of light.

"Supposing I had ... not seen ... him?" she asked in a low whisper.

"But you did! And I shall not die—not today at any rate!"

Her fingers tightened on his.

"Do not ... speak like that," she pleaded. "I ... I cannot ... bear it."

"I am not afraid to die," the Prince replied. "In fact I was thinking when I was in the Abbey that it would be easier to die than to live without you."

His words made the tears come into her eyes.

As she tried to blink them away, she told herself that she should not be crying as she had last night, but smiling, because, despite all their resolutions to keep away from each other, they were together again.

The Prince raised her hand to his lips and she felt his mouth not hard, passionate, and violent as it had been last night, but soft, gentle, and at the same time possessive.

"I tried to tell myself that I was wise and sensible not to see you again," he said in a very low voice which could not be overheard by the servants in front of them, "but now you are here and nothing else seems to matter."

"You told me not to ... watch you going to the Coronation and coming back," Angelina said, "but I had to."

"It was very fortunate for me that you did."

"How could anyone want to ... kill you?" she asked. "I saw last night how much your people love you."

"Revolutionaries seldom have good reasons for what they do," the Prince replied lightly. "They just want to overthrow the existing order."

He smiled at her as he added:

"You see, there are dangers even in my mountainous Paradise."

"You must take ... care of yourself."

148

He did not reply, but she felt that metaphorically he shrugged his shoulders.

"Please," she pleaded, "for my . . . sake."

"If you ask me like that, you know I have to do as you wish," he answered, "but as I have already said, I am not afraid of dying."

"You have to live," Angelina answered. "I feel it is imperative for you to live, not only for your own sake but for Greece."

The Prince sighed.

"I feel I am doing enough for my country in giving you up," he said. "They surely cannot ask further sacrifice of me?"

Angelina did not speak for a moment, then she said:

"I was thinking last night, when I was crying in my misery at losing you, that once in history Greece changed the thinking of the world, and that is what it must do again."

The Prince smiled.

"I know what you are saying to me," he said. "That was the time when men were only a little lower than gods."

"And that is what they must be again."

"The Greeks have forgotten the vision they had then," the Prince said.

"Then you must make them remember," Angelina said. "You, and everybody who thinks like you, must bring the ideals and the splendour that was Greece back to a world that is badly in need of it."

The Prince looked down into her face and his eyes were very tender.

"Only you, my precious, could think like that," he said. "Only you could think, as a Greek would, that holiness lay in the beauty which they found everywhere they looked."

Once again he raised her hand to his lips, and said:

"We think alike, we are alike, and it is difficult for

me to think of you except as a Greek, with a Greek's imagination of what the world needs."

Angelina gave him a little smile.

"I have something to tell you . . ."

Then as she spoke, she realised that Captain Soutsos was standing beside the carriage.

"It is all right now, Sir," he said to the Prince. "We caught the man."

"Who was he?"

"A Turk!"

"A Turk?" the Prince exclaimed. "Are you sure?"

"He is not being very communicative at the moment," Captain Soutsos said with a slight smile. "We were somewhat rough with him! But I glanced at the papers in his pocket and they were written in Turkish and there is no doubt from his appearance what his origins are."

"I cannot understand what he has to gain from killing me."

"Perhaps we shall learn more when he recovers consciousness," Captain Soutsos said drily.

He looked at Angelina.

"We owe you a great debt of gratitude, Miss Medwin. The assailant, whatever his nationality, carried a very accurate and high-powered rifle. His Royal Highness would not have had a chance of survival."

Angelina gave a little cry and the Prince said:

"Get in, Aristotelis. I will not have Miss Medwin upset, but I am sure His Excellency would wish to thank her."

"He is very anxious to do so," Captain Soutsos replied. Angelina felt that she should protest and say that it was best for her to remain anonymous. But she knew that was impossible. Captain Soutsos had already told the Minister that she had informed them of the danger to the Prince.

Captain Soutsos sat opposite them.

"I should have told you there was another man with

him," Angelina said, remembering that she had not told the Prince about the man in the mackintosh. "He kicked Twi-Twi when he barked, which was how I found out there was a man hidden in the bushes with a gun."

"Another man!" Captain Soutsos ejaculated. "You will have to be very careful, Sir."

The Prince did not answer, and Alexis drew up the horses with a flourish at the front door of the Ministry.

The Prince got out first and helped Angelina onto the red carpet. Without waiting to be lifted from the carriage, Twi-Twi followed them and jumped down onto the ground.

As she walked up the steps Angelina looked at him apprehensively, knowing that if he saw the ginger cat he would rush after it like a streak of lightning.

At the same time, it was really Twi-Twi who had saved the Prince and he was entitled to his glorious hour as she was to hers.

Waiting in the Hall was the Minister. He was flanked on either side by officials in their magnificent diplomatic uniforms and behind them a crowd of what appeared to be the entire staff of the Ministry.

As the Prince appeared there was an outburst of clapping and cheers as there had been the night before, but Angelina thought they were more subdued and more refined than the exuberant Cephalonians in the Restaurant.

"Your Royal Highness," the Minister said, "I can only thank God that your life has been spared, and I ask Miss Medwin to accept on behalf of myself and everyone present our most sincere and heart-felt thanks that she was instrumental in saving you."

There was another outburst of applause, and as Angelina put out her hand the Minister raised it to his lips.

"May I present my colleagues to you, Miss Medwin," he said, "who wish to add their grateful thanks to mine."

Angelina smiled rather shyly.

"First let me introduce the Prime Minister of Cephalonia," the Minister said, "Mr. Alexandros Ypsilantis."

"You are the saviour of our most beloved Ruler, Miss Medwin," the Prime Minister said.

"And now," the Minister went on, "Mr. Kharilaos Costas, the Foreign Minister."

Before he could complete the word, Twi-Twi, who had been keeping close beside Angelina as if slightly overawed by such a crowd of people, started to bark furiously at the man standing next to the Prime Minister.

Angelina looked at him apologetically, and as she did so she saw that he was the man she had seen getting into the second carriage which had been driven away to the Abbey.

Mr. Costas frowned as he looked down at Twi-Twi and moved his legs in their black silk stockings somewhat uncomfortably. Suddenly it flashed through Angelina's mind that she had seen him more than once.

Incredibly, she thought she must be mistaken—she realised that the man in the garden who had hurried away after kicking Twi-Twi had, beneath his black mackintosh, been wearing silk stockings!

She had at that moment been so angry over Twi-Twi being hurt that she had not consciously noticed anything except the swiftness with which the man had let himself out through the gate.

Now she knew, as Twi-Twi did, who had been hidden in the bushes and in fact directing the gunman waiting to assassinate the Prince.

Twi-Twi was working himself up into a furious passion, barking ferociously and making menacing little runs at the man facing him as if he would bury his sharp white teeth in one of his legs.

Just for a moment Angelina thought he was going to kick Twi-Twi again, and without considering the consequences she cried out:

"That is the man! That is the man I saw in the bushes talking to the assassin with the rifle!"

Her voice rang out in the high-ceilinged Hall and the Prince turned his head to look at her in sheer astonishment.

Then, before anybody could speak, the Foreign Minister drew a pistol from his pocket and pointed it at the Prince.

"Yes, it was I!" he said. "And you had all better get out of my way unless you want your reigning Prince to die in front of your eyes!"

His pistol was pointed at the Prince's heart as he started to edge his way slowly through the men round him towards the door.

It seemed as if everyone was paralysed into immobility, until Twi-Twi made a wild dash and buried his teeth in a black silk-stockinged leg.

The Foreign Minister gave an involuntary cry which turned into an oath, and looked down at his small attacker, preparing to kick him out of his way again.

In that split second the Prince moved.

He flung himself at the Foreign Minister and forced his hand holding the revolver up into the air.

There was the resounding explosion of a shot, which was quickly followed by another one, and Angelina saw Kharilaos Costas stagger and collapse on the ground.

Captain Soutsos had shot him while he was grappling with the Prince.

There was a sudden movement as everyone surged forward, and as Angelina stood rooted to the ground, she felt the Prince's arms go round her as he half-carried her out of the Hall and into another room.

He pushed the door shut behind them and held Angelina close against him.

She was too shocked, too stunned by everything that had happened, to do anything but hold on to him, her face turned up to his, her eyes searching as if to see if he was really alive, really safe after all.

"It is all right, my precious," he said, "and now, thanks to you, I know who my enemy was."

"You . . . said you . . . did not . . . l-like him," Angelina murmured incoherently.

"And how right I was! He must have been intriguing with the Turks to take over the island and must have been instigating the demonstrations and riots for which the Prime Minister and I could not account."

"You are alive! You are . . . alive!" Angelina cried.

"I am alive, my darling one," the Prince replied, "but it is not right to involve you in such horrors."

His lips found hers and he kissed her passionately and almost frantically, as if it were she rather than himself who had been in danger.

He took off her hat and threw it on the ground and went on kissing her until the room swung round her and she was caught up in the magic enchantment she had thought she would never know again.

The door behind them opened a little way and someone—Angelina guessed that it was Captain Soutsos—pushed Two-Twi into the room.

He was not barking at anyone but intrigued and curious, as Pekingese always are, on finding himself somewhere new, and he started to explore the room.

Angelina gave a weak little laugh.

"I did not . . . save you," she said. "It was Twi-Twi! He recognised the Foreign Minister . . . because he had kicked him in the garden!"

"That is the kind of thing the swine would do," the Prince said, "but forget about him."

As he spoke, he drew Angelina towards the sofa that was beside the fireplace, filled with flowers.

She saw, as she moved, that she was in a very large

154

room, and because there was a big table in the middle
of it, she guessed it was used as the Council Chamber.

At the end of the table was a magnificently carved
chair bearing the Cephalonian coat-of-arms, which she
felt was really a throne.

It made her remember that the Prince was Royal
and that because of it, they were forced to say good-
bye to each other.

Yet it was difficult to think of anything at this moment except that the Prince was beside her and his
face was near to hers.

"I love you!" he said as they sat down together. "My
precious little Persephone, I love you, and no-one
could be more courageous. But I am going to get you
something to drink."

"I do not want . . . anything," Angelina protested.

The Prince paid no attention and walked across the
room to where there was a table set with glasses and
several crystal decanters.

"A glass of wine is what we both need," he said
firmly as he poured it out.

Angelina felt that he was speaking for the sake of
speaking and they were both thinking that in a short
time she would have to leave him again.

Because he looked so magnificent and so impressive
in the uniform he had worn for the Coronation, she
wanted to run to his side and ask him to hold her in
his arms and kiss her again.

'I must behave properly,' she thought, and forced
herself to look away from him.

Glancing up over the mantlepiece, she saw a large
portrait.

As the Prince joined her, a glass in each of his hands,
she remarked:

"How strange that you should have a picture of
Lord Byron here!"

"Why strange?" he asked. "My cousin would not

think a Cephalonian Ministry or a Greek Embassy
complete unless it contained a portrait of the man to
whom, more than anyone else, we owe our freedom."

"Do you mean Lord Byron?" Angelina questioned.

"But of course!" the Prince replied. "I thought you
were a student of our history."

"I try to be," Angelina answered, "but personally I
think of Lord Byron in a very ... different way."

She took the glass from the Prince as she spoke, and
added:

"I was just going to tell you, because you said I
thought like a ... Greek, that I am in fact Lord Byron's ... great granddaughter."

She spoke with a little smile on her lips, feeling that
if the portrait was hung in the Ministry, the Prince
would not be shocked as she had been afraid he might
be.

But when she looked up at him, he was staring at her
with a very strange expression on his face.

"What are you saying?" he asked. "I do not understand."

"I wanted to tell you when we first met," Angelina
said, "how it is that I have Greek blood in my veins,
but I thought you would be shocked. Papa has always
told me that I was not to mention it to anybody."

"Mention what?"

"That my grandmother was Lord Byron's daughter."

The Prince sat down beside Angelina on the sofa.

"Start from the beginning," he said. "How do you
know that? How can that be true?"

Angelina looked at him anxiously.

"Are ... are you ... shocked?" she asked. "I ... did
not think you ... would be."

"I am not shocked, my darling," the Prince replied,
"I am only waiting to hear something which I can
hardly believe, hardly credit is not just a part of your
imagination."

"It is true!" Angelina exclaimed.

She looked up at Lord Byron's picture and thought his handsome face was encouraging her as she said:

"When he was staying in Cephalonia for the four months before he went to Missolonghi, where he died, he fell very much ... in love with a ... beautiful Cephalonion girl."

"How is it possible that we did not know this?" the Prince asked.

"Because," Angelina said, "she came from an important family."

"Do you know the name?"

"Yes ... it was Diliyiannis."

"I know them! Of course I know them!" the Prince exclaimed.

"She and Lord Byron met secretly, and he wrote her some very beautiful letters and of course ... some poems."

"You have them?"

"Papa put them in the Bank for safety, and also because he was afraid that I might show them to somebody."

"Go on!" the Prince said. "Tell me everything—everything!"

He spoke with an insistence that Angelina thought was rather surprising, but she continued in a low voice:

"After Lord Byron left Cephalonia, Nonika, for that was her name ... realised that she was ... having a ... baby."

Angelina blushed as she spoke.

Even though she was very proud of her connection with Lord Byron, it was embarrassing to speak of such things to the Prince.

As if he understood what she was feeling, he put out his hand and took hers, holding it very closely.

"Nonika was therefore forced to tell her family how

157

much she had loved Lord Byron," Angelina went on. "They were horrified that she should be in ... trouble, and they were ... determined to keep it ... secret."

"The baby was born in Cephalonia?" the Prince asked.

"Yes. It was a girl, and she was christened Athene by a Priest who was sworn to secrecy."

"What happened then?"

"Lord Byron had become great friends with the British Governor and Military Resident Colonel Charles James Napier."

"I remember that," the Prince said.

"He also loved a Cephalonion, who was called Anastasia, and they had two daughters."

"That is true," the Prince murmured.

"As soon as she was old enough to travel, Colonal Napier took Athene to England and she was brought up by one of his relatives."

Angelina smiled as she continued:

"When she was twenty she fell very much in love with Henry Medwin, who was a Captain in the Grenadier Guards. They had two little daughters who died in infancy, and then my father was born in 1855."

She paused for a moment and said wistfully:

"I never knew my grandmother because she died when I was only a year old, and then Grandpapa married again."

She glanced up at the Prince and went on:

"Because Papa wished it, I have always called his Step-mother 'Grandmama.' He never speaks of his real mother."

Her fingers tightened on the Prince's as she said:

"Please, tell ... me you are not ... shocked. The Medwin family have always been very ashamed of what they think of as 'a skeleton in the cupboard,' but I have always been proud, very proud to be a relative of Lord Byron."

"Of course you are!" the Prince exclaimed. "And,

my darling, surely you understand that this changes everything?"

Angelina looked at him, not understanding.

"I mean," he said gently, "that now we can be married—if you will accept me, my precious little Persephone!"

"M-married?" Angelina said "But how? I do not understand. You have to marry somebody Royal."

"It would be far more acceptable for me to marry Byron's great-granddaughter," he said. "Everyone knows that he was to have been offered the Sovereignty of Greece at Salona, and certainly the Greeks regarded him then, as now, as a King among men."

"I . . . did not know," Angelina said. "Is that . . . true?"

"Absolutely true, as any Greek will tell you," the Prince answered. "But most of all he belongs to us— the Cephalonians. I cannot imagine anything that would give my people more pleasure than for me to marry the descendant of a man who is looked on not only as a saviour of Greece but also on the island as almost a Saint."

"I . . . cannot believe it!" Angelina cried.

"I see that your knowledge of history, my darling, is somewhat inadequate!" the Prince said with a smile.

Then he went on in a more serious vein:

"The fall of Missolonghi in 1826 would have been just one more horror of war, except that two years earlier Lord Byron had given his life for Greece."

His voice deepened as he continued:

"The tragic fall of Missolonghi shocked Europe. But for Byron's death, the Turkish Fleet might never have been attacked and destroyed in the bay of Navarino the following year, and the last flicker of Greek freedom might have been extinguished."

Angelina clasped her hands together.

"I remember . . . now."

"Fifty-seven of the Turkish war-ships were sunk,"

the Prince said, "by twenty-six British, French, and Russians."

He looked up at Byron's portrait before he said:

"By the end of the century Greece had slowly gathered herself together as a nation. Byron's faith in Greek unity, to which few paid any attention in his lifetime, became in his death an idea of immense credibility."

"I think ... I understand," Angelina whispered.

"What the Greeks said, and indeed the rest of the world," the Prince said solemnly, "was that if Lord Byron, the most famous figure in Europe, had chosen to link his name with strife-torn, down-trodden, 'poor Greece,' hers must indeed be a cause worth fighting for."

The Prince rose to his feet and drew Angelina to hers.

With his arm round her, he lifted his glass towards the picture over the mantelpiece.

"It is because of you," he said quietly, "that my people and I are free. It is because of you that I shall find happiness with your great-granddaughter. Together we will continue your fight for the ideals of Greece—which will never die!"

# Chapter Seven

The Prince put out his hand to help Angelina up a stony path that was shadowed by trees.

They had left their horses with Captain Soutsos at the bottom of the incline, and now Twi-Twi, who had been carried in a saddle-bag on the Captain's horse, ran ahead of them.

His white tail was arched over his back as if he were leading a small crusade on his own.

"This is very exciting!" Angelina exclaimed.

The Prince smiled at her with such tenderness in his eyes that she felt as if the sunshine blazed through the thickness of the leaves above them.

They had only been married for ten days, but they had planned that their first pilgrimage would be to Metaxata, which had been the name of Byron's island retreat in Cephalonia.

To Angelina it was astonishing that Lord Byron, who in England was still considered to be a libertine, should be respected and revered with awe by the Greeks, who believed him to be both heroic and holy.

From the moment she had arrived in Cephalonia, she had known that the Prince had been right in describing it as a mountainous Paradise, and it was even more beautiful than she had expected it to be.

The air quivered with a brilliant yet soft light which

seemed to be concentrated with a dazzling radiance on the mountain-peaks.

At times Angelina felt that she herself had become a goddess and that the Prince was in fact Apollo, as she had first imagined him to be.

It still seemed incredible that simply because her great-grandfather was Lord Byron, her misery and unhappiness had been swept away from the moment she had looked up at his portrait in the Cephalonian Ministry and told the Prince her secret.

Sometimes in the night she would wake up thinking that her happiness was all a dream and she, in obedience to her father, had not told the Prince the secret of her grandmother's birth.

She had begun to realise how important the revelation of her secret was to be, when the Prince, standing in front of Lord Byron's portrait, had kissed her until she was breathless, then had gone to the door.

With a note of irrepressible excitement in his voice, he had told one of the servants in the Hall to ask the Minister and everyone else who was with him to come into the Council Chamber.

Angelina had watched him a little apprehensively until he joined her again, then she put out her hands and asked nervously:

"What . . . are you going . . . to do?"

"I am going to introduce my future wife to my Prime Minister, who has been so concerned over my marriage," he replied.

"Are you . . . sure . . . quite sure that it will be . . . all right for you to . . . marry me?"

"I am going to marry you," he answered; "and do not forget that as you saved my life, I am your responsibility from now on."

"That is . . . all I want," Angelina said, "but I would not . . . wish to do anything that was not entirely right for your . . . country."

"Marrying you will not only be the right thing to do,

but it will be just the inspiration which Cephalonia needs," the Prince said positively.

The Minister, looking a little shaken from what had just taken place, came filing into the room with the Prime Minister and all the other officials.

Angelina thought shyly that they would suppose the Prince had sent for them so that they could thank her again for being instrumental not only in saving the Prince's life but also in disclosing the villain in their midst.

The Prince waited until they were all inside the room. Then as the door shut he said:

"Gentlemen, I have such an important announcement to make that I know you will feel as I do—surprise and yet at the same time an irrepressible elation."

He paused for a moment; then, taking Angelina's hand in his, he said:

"You have already met Miss Medwin. You know how courageous she had been and what she has already done for us, but what you do not know is that she is in fact the great-granddaughter of the man we revere above all others, Lord Byron, who died for us when nobody else in the world was interested."

As he spoke, the Prince looked up at Lord Byron's portrait, and Angelina, watching the Statesmen's eyes follow his, could see the astonishment in their expression and something which seemed almost an adoration.

This, she was to learn when she reached Cephalonia, was the right word.

The memory of Lord Byron was adored, and in the little village of Metaxata she was shown a great ivy which was said to have been planted by him, and at the beginning of the path they were climbing now was a rough wooden signpost bearing the words: *"Byron's Roci."*

When she talked to the Cephalonians they all

seemed to quote Byron's words and his poems as if it was a part of their everyday conversation.

It was not only as the Prince's bride that everyone wished to meet her or to cheer her as she moved about the Capital, but also because her blood was part of theirs.

Everything had happened so quickly that by the time Angelina arrived in Cephalonia she felt, as the ship sailed into the harbour, that she was breathless from the haste in which everything had taken place.

The Prince had been so insistent in his desire to marry her as quickly as possible that even Lady Medwin had not protested.

She was in fact so thrilled at the prospect of Angelina being a reigning Princess that she even forgot to rebuke her for being deceitful in having met the Prince without telling her.

Neither Angelina nor the Prince revealed the fact that they had dined alone together or had attended the Cephalonian party at the Restaurant.

They just admitted to having been introduced by Twi-Twi and the ginger cat, and having met in the garden.

Immersed in the excitement of providing Angelina with a trousseau in under three weeks and arranging for her to travel to Cephalonia, where she was to be married, Lady Medwin fortunately did not ask too many searching questions.

The Prince in fact smoothed everything over and was so charming to Lady Medwin that she confessed to Angelina:

"He is the most delightful young man I have ever met—in fact I am in love with him myself!"

Unfortunately, although all the excitement revived Lady Medwin's health, she was not well enough to travel with Angelina to her wedding.

Lady Hewlett came to the rescue, declaring that it would give her the greatest possible pleasure to visit

Cephalonia, and as it would be impossible for Angelina's father to return from India in time to give her away, Lord Hewlett would be only too delighted to deputise for him.

Because Angelina knew how disappointed her grandmother was that she could not attend her wedding, she told her over and over again how much she would have liked her to be there.

But it was the Prince who, before he left England, insisted that Lady Medwin was well enough to have a Reception in the big Drawing-Room which had been shrouded in its Holland covers for so long.

"It will be too much for her!" Angelina protested when they were alone.

"Nonsense!" the Prince replied. "Happiness and excitement never killed anyone. It is when people are bored and disillusioned that they die."

He had seen the indecision in Angelina's face and kissed her, adding:

"That is something, my darling, which will never happen to either of us. You will excite and entrance me until my dying day."

"I ... hope so," Angelina replied in a small voice, "but you have seen so much and done so many things in your life ... while I was still at School ... and at times I feel very ignorant."

"Wherever you have been," the Prince said, "you have thought, and we agree it is thought, that the Greeks brought to the world an appreciation of beauty."

He kissed her again and added:

"That is something you have, my darling, in abundance, and you are so beautiful that I am content to spend the next thousand years just looking at you."

*　　*　　*

When Lady Medwin, dressed in her best gown and wearing all her jewellery, was carried down the stairs

165

to the Drawing-Room where she received her guests, sitting comfortably in a chair with an ermine rug over her knees, Angelina knew that the Prince had been right.

'As he always is,' she thought to herself, 'and I have so much to learn from him.'

It appeared that almost everybody in London wanted to meet Prince Xenos and the girl who was to be his English bride.

But as it was impossible to accommodate them all, they were obliged to restrict the invitations to Lady Medwin's personal friends and the Prince's Royal and diplomatic connections who could not be left out.

It was a delight in itself for Angelina to see the Drawing-Room looking as it was meant to look, with the chandeliers sparkling and the room fragrant with the scent of lilies.

Angelina's gown, made at break-neck speed which entailed the staff of the dressmaker who had designed it having to sit up all night to get it finished in time, was, the Prince told her, a poem in itself.

"You look like Aphrodite," he said, and added when they were alone: "To the Greeks, the goddess of love was not a many-breasted matron but a young virgin rising out of the sea."

His lips were very near to Angelina's as he added:

"Beautiful, my precious one, and full of promise like the coming of a new day."

"That is what our ... marriage will be," Angelina whispered, "a new day ... and we shall be ... together."

\* \* \*

After the Reception, the Prince had left for Cephalonia to make all the necessary preparations for their wedding.

The Prime Minister had gone with him, and the

newly appointed Foreign Minister was to be one of Angelina's escorts, as was Captain Soutsos.

It was the Aide-de-Camp who on the journey took charge of Twi-Twi.

At the last moment, seeing how much Angelina minded leaving the little white Pekingese behind, Lady Medwin had given her Twi-Twi.

"Do you really mean it, Grandmama?" Angelina had exclaimed. "I would rather have Twi-Twi than all the many wonderful gifts I have received, but I would not like you to be unhappy without him."

"I think, dearest child, that he would be unhappy without you," Lady Medwin replied, "and I am really too old to have a dog, because I cannot look after him properly."

She smiled and added:

"Who will take him to the garden if you are not there? Although I assure you I would make the effort if I thought I could meet anyone so delightful as dear Xenos!"

"They say lightning never strikes twice in the same place!" Angelina replied with a laugh.

When she went to bed that night she hugged Twi-Twi and said:

"I am so glad you are coming with me, and if people look at me with curiosity, they will certainly think you are a visitor from another planet!"

It was true that Twi-Twi caused so much interest that Angelina really felt she ought to have him in her wedding-procession, but instead she was provided with ten very beautiful young women who were to be her bridesmaids.

They came from all the most important families in Cephalonia and the name of the two leading bridesmaids was Diliyiannis.

These two girls were in fact so lovely that Angelina was glad that in contrast to their dark beauty, she was fair-haired and blue-eyed.

"I cannot think," she said to the Prince after they were married, "why you did not fall in love with a Cephalonian. I cannot imagine that any woman anywhere could be more lovely."

"I can give you a lot of sensible answers to that question," he replied, "but instead I will spoil you by saying I have never really been in love until I met you."

"I can hardly believe that is true," Angelina said.

She thought it was impossible for such a handsome, attractive man to go through the world for twenty-eight years without having hundreds of women in love with him.

But the Prince, knowing what she was thinking, as he always did, said:

"I am not straining your credulity. I have been attracted, amused, and beguiled by quite a number of lovely ladies here, in Paris, and once in London. But when I saw Persephone she walked straight into my heart, and I knew that I had never known love until that moment."

"Oh, Xenos!" Angelina said softly. "You say such ... wonderful things to me, I am beginning to think that every ... Cephalonian man is a poet at heart."

"If you mean that they will speak to you as I do," the Prince said, "then I shall not only be extremely jealous, but will shut you up in the Palace and see that no-one comes near you except myself!"

"That is a very Turkish way of thinking," Angelina teased.

The Prince pulled her into his arms and kissed her fiercely and passionately until she apologised.

"If you call me a Turk," he threatened, "I shall behave like one."

But she was in fact pleased to find that he could be jealous, as she knew it would be impossible not to be jealous of him.

Everything about him and the island itself had a

magic quality that made her thank God not once but a thousand times a day that she had been privileged to know such happiness.

The deep green valleys, and the sides of the mountains covered with pine, myrtle, lavender, and sage, were more beautiful, the Prince told her, at this time of the year than at any other.

Today they had seen handsome mahogany-skinned peasants carrying loads of wood or the last baskets of grapes from the vines.

It was very hot even for September, and it had been a delight to move from the heat down near the sea up into the mountains to Metaxata.

Angelina had been shown where, standing at the window of his Villa, her great-grandfather had written of "this beautiful village" from which he could see in the "calm though cool serenity" of "transparent moonlight" the "distant outline of Morea between the double azure of the waves and the sky."

Below his small Villa, Byron had seen the dark green of the orange and lemon trees, the yellowing pines as Angelina saw them now, the grey olives, and the blue water dotted with green or misty islands.

Having visited Metaxata, the Prince had told her that they must ride to the nearest village, Lakythra, and after a delicious luncheon of Greek dishes, they had set off escorted only by Captain Soutsos and Twi-Twi.

The Prince had not told Angelina what to expect but she had read her great-grandfather's journals and everything that had been written about him.

She was therefore not surprised when at the end of the path they climbed again to where, on a hill, there was a little white Chapel and a group of flat grey rocks lying on the green turf, with a glorious view of the sea.

"Now I know why you brought me here," Angelina cried as they reached the summit. "It was on these rocks, with a breath-taking view below him, that Great-Grandpapa sat writing."

Holding the Prince's hand, she looked out over the country below them and in the distance the vivid blue sea.

Very softly she quoted:

"*'If I am a poet I owe it to the air of Greece.'*"

The Prince kissed her hand. Then he took off his hat as if to feel the cool air with its strange light in it on his forehead.

There was an expression on his face which made Angelina think of the moment when they had been married in the Cathedral and he had repeated his vows in a voice that was so deep and so sincere with meaning that she had felt the tears come into her eyes.

She had felt then as if her whole being rose in a paean of gratitude because she had been privileged to meet such a wonderful man.

She was deeply, inexpressibly grateful because their love for each other had finally triumphed over what had at first seemed insurmountable difficulties.

She knew in herself, and she told the Prince so, that she would have loved him whoever he had been, and if the choice had only been hers, nothing would have prevented her from marrying him.

"I know that, my precious," he replied.

That night after the wedding-ceremony, when he had come to her room, she had thought there was something god-like about him and that he was in fact Apollo, with whom she had identified him.

She had been waiting for him, not in the big bed with its headboard carved like a silver shell from the sea, but standing at the window looking out onto the sea, above which the stars were gradually filling the sable of the night with twinkling brilliance.

Already their reflection was glimmering on the soft-moving water and Angelina knew that soon there would be the silver rays of the rising moon and the pale limpid light of the Milky Way.

Everything was quiet and still and the very darkness had in it a mysterious magic which was part of her love.

She heard the Prince come across the room behind her and she turned to smile at him, not realising that her fair hair was faintly lit by the stars so that it seemed to halo her head.

The Prince reached her but did not touch her, he only stood looking at her face, and for Angelina there was no need for words.

The ceremony which had taken place in the Cathedral, the crowds at the Reception which had followed, the cheers from those who had watched them drive to the Palace in an open carriage, had all faded into oblivion.

Now the only thing that mattered was that they were alone, just she and the Prince.

This was the moment they had been waiting for, and it seemed as if everything that had happened had been like the raising of a curtain on the drama of their souls.

"Are you real?" the Prince asked, and his voice was deep.

"I ... love you!" Angelina answered.

"That is what I wanted you to say," he replied, "and yet I find it hard to believe that you are mine and that I need never again be afraid I might lose you."

"It does not ... seem as if it could have ... happened ... but it has!" Angelina said. "I am ... here and ... I am your wife!"

"Do you suppose I do not realise that?" the Prince asked. "Because I have wanted you so intensely, Angelina, I feel as if I have moved the very heavens to gain you and the gods have given you to me."

"How could we ... feel anything else ... when the

171

gods are ... so near?" Angelina asked. "I can feel them in the air ... and see them everywhere I look."

There was a note in her voice which made the Prince put out his arms and pull her against him, not roughly, not violently, but gently, as if she was something infinitely precious that he treasured, so that he was touching it with tender fingers.

Angelina put her head against his shoulder, then looked out to sea.

She knew that even in the dark, there was always a glimmer of light; the light that was Greece, the light that also came from the Prince, which was part of their love.

Just for a moment she felt as if they were one half of the celestial beauty of the world.

Then the Prince's arms tightened round her and he turned her face up to his. At the touch of his lips she could no longer think or see, but only feel that as their love quivered round them with silver wings, they were both Divine.

\* \* \*

Now looking, as her great-grandfather had looked, over the valley below, standing where he had stood, and feeling that he had played his part in bringing her such happiness, Angelina said:

"I think this place tells you, darling Xenos, as it tells me, that we have to work not only for Cephalonia but for the ... whole of Greece."

"That is what I hoped you would think," the Prince said. "Greece needs us. There is still disunity, still dissension, still the Turks have a foothold in Crete."

"And yet, since my great-grandfather died in Missolonghi so much has been accomplished," Angelina said, with a little sigh of satisfaction.

She turned round after she had spoken and looked at the little white Chapel.

"Is it open?"

The Prince shook his head.

"They suggested they should notify the Priests, who only worship there on Sundays, that we were coming," he said, "but I wanted to be here with you alone."

"That is what I would have wanted if you had asked me," Angelina said. "Oh, Xenos, how can you plan so that everything we do is always so perfect?"

"It is quite simple," the Prince replied. "I think of what you would want, and strangely enough, it is exactly what I want myself!"

Angelina laughed, then she said:

"Look at Twi-Twi. He has explored the flat rocks and now he is exploring the entrance to the Chapel."

"There is a little exploring I want to do," the Prince said.

He drew Angelina off the flat grey rocks to where beyond them, away from the Chapel, there were thick shrubs and twisted vines interspersed with other greenery.

Growing amongst them were some of the exquisitely beautiful flowers which had delighted Angelina ever since she had arrived on the island.

They moved amongst them and found another view, this time of the mountains and the tall cypress trees which stood like sentinels.

"It is . . . all so . . . lovely!"

Angelina breathed rather than spoke the words.

The Prince put his arms round her.

"And so are you, my beautiful wife!"

They were standing under the shade of a tree and he undid the ribbons which tied her wide-brimmed hat under her chin.

"I want to kiss you," he said, "and make sure that you will not fly away into the air, leaving me merely dreaming—doubting that you ever existed."

"I am very real, my darling," she replied.

173

He threw her hat on the soft grass on which they were standing and pulled off his own coat. Then he held out his arms and she melted against him.

It had been too hot to wear anything but her coolest muslin gown for the climb to the flat stones.

Now through the fineness of his white lawn shirt she could feel the Prince's heart beating against hers.

"You are mine!" he said. "Mine, my precious little Persephone, and every day I find myself falling more and more in love with you."

"I find the same with you," she replied. "I think it is impossible to love you more, and yet at ... night, when we are ... alone together, I find there are new ... depths to my love and new feelings that ... at this moment I cannot imagine."

"I make you happy?"

"Not only ... happy ... but wildly, thrillingly rapturous ... like touching the tops of your marvellous mountains ... and diving down into the depths of your blue, blue sea."

"My sweet little goddess, that is how I want you to feel."

Angelina put her lips close to his ear.

"Making love ..." she whispered, "is the most ... perfect, beautiful ... thing I could ever imagine."

The Prince bent his head to kiss her neck and she felt a streak of light flash through her, half-ecstasy, half-pain.

"Please ... darling," she pleaded, "do ... not ... excite me like that until ... tonight."

The Prince's arms tightened. Then he asked:

"Why should we wait for tonight?"

He lifted her off her feet as he spoke and laid her down, with her head on his coat, on the soft grasses in the shadow of the tree that loomed above them.

Angelina gave a little cry.

"Xenos! Supposing somebody should see us?"

"If anyone should try to come near us," the Prince

replied, "our sentinel will not only warn us but will see them off!"

For a moment Angelina did not know what he meant. Then she saw that Twi-Twi was lying a little way from them, apparently looking out at the view, but she was quite certain that Twi-Twi was alert and watchful.

She gave a little laugh.

"Yes, Twi-Twi will warn us," she said, "and I think he knows that the fact that I am here and we are married is all ... due to him."

"He was undoubtedly sent to us by the gods," the Prince said, "and who am I to refuse anything they should offer?"

But he was not speaking of Twi-Twi as his lips found Angelina's and she felt his hand hard and insistent through the softness of her gown.

"You are not only the most beautiful person I have ever seen," he said in his deep voice, "but you excite me as I have never been excited before."

"Is that ... really true?" Angelina asked. "I feel so ignorant about love ... will you teach me ... about it?"

The Prince smiled.

"What do you think I am doing now, my adorable, enticing little wife?"

As he spoke he had undone the buttons which fastened the front of her dress and now his hand was on her heart.

"Oh, Xenos!"

She felt rising within her the fires which he had ignited in her the first night they were married and which had burned more fiercely, more irresistibly, every night since.

Just for a moment her mind went back to the past and she thought that perhaps on this very spot Lord Byron had met Nonika and they had made love as she and Xenos were doing now.

Perhaps it was in this particular place that Athene had been conceived.

It was because Athene had married her grandfather that she had not only Greek but Byron's blood in her veins and she was the wife of Xenos.

It was all such a marvellous, incredible story and one day she would tell it to her own children.

She prayed now that Xenos might give her a baby who would be beautiful because it was part of the love that shimmered all round them, and the love which Byron had given to Nonika.

"I want you," Xenos was saying hoarsely. "My precious, I want you now, at this moment."

Then it was impossible for the moment to think of anything but him.

Angelina felt herself quiver against him and knew the fire was rising like a flame up through her body and into her lips.

The desire which vibrated between them made her feel that they burned with the light of the sun.

"I love you ... I love you!" she cried.

She was not certain whether she spoke the words aloud, but they came spontaneously from the new sensations, the new wonder, and a new ecstasy she had never known before.

Then, as Xenos made her his, they were one with the shimmering, crystallised light of their magical, mountainous Paradise.

*Author's Note*

In 1973 the British Byron Society asked the Mayor of Missolonghi if the people of his town could join with them in celebrating the 150th anniversary of the poet's death.

"But he is not your Lord Byron, he is *our* Lord Byron," the Mayor protested.

At Lakythra a glittering white marble slab on the largest grey stone rock bears the inscription in Greek capitals: "*If I am a poet I owe it to the air of Greece —Byron.*"

In Athens, where Byron's monument stands in the corner of the Zappeion Gardens in direct line with the Parthenon, Helles crowns him with laurels.

At Missolonghi in the "Garden of Heroes," above his coat-of-arms is a Royal Crown.

In the light which permeates every rock and wave of Greece, Byron said on his death-bed: "My wealth, my abilities, I devoted to her cause—well, there is my life to her."

But his death brought life to Greece and eventually freedom.

Everything I have written about Cephalonia is true, except that I have given them a Royal Family. It is what I feel they deserve.

Twi-Twi* is my own White Lion Pekingese. He is a descendant of the Alderbourne strain, the finest in the world, which started in 1904.

He is proud, intrepid, authoritative, imperious, in fact—Imperially Royal.

*Pronounced Ti-Ti.

## ABOUT THE AUTHOR

BARBARA CARTLAND, the world's most famous romantic novelist, who is also an historian, playwright, lecturer, political speaker and television personality, has now written over 200 books. She has also had many historical works published and has written four autobiographies as well as the biographies of her mother and that of her brother Ronald Cartland, who was the first Member of Parliament to be killed in the last war. This book has a preface by Sir Winston Churchill. Barbara Cartland has sold 80 million books over the world, more than half of these in the U.S.A. She broke the world record in 1975 by writing twenty books, and her own record in 1976 with twenty-one. In private life, Barbara Cartland, who is a Dame of the Order of St. John of Jerusalem, has fought for better conditions and salaries for Midwives and Nurses. As President of the Royal College of Midwives (Hertfordshire Branch), she has been invested with the first Badge of Office ever given in Great Britain, which was subscribed to by the Midwives themselves. She has also championed-the-cause for old people and founded the first Romany Gypsy Camp in the world. Barbara Cartland is deeply interested in Vitamin Therapy and is President of the British National Association for Health.

# BARBARA CARTLAND
## PRESENTS
## THE ANCIENT WISDOM SERIES

The world's all-time bestselling author of romantic fiction, Barbara Cartland, has established herself as High Priestess of Love in its purest and most traditionally romantic form.

"We have," she says, "in the last few years thrown out the spiritual aspect of love and concentrated only on the crudest and most debased sexual side.

"Love at its highest has inspired mankind since the beginning of time. Civilization's greatest pictures, music, prose and poetry have all been written under the influence of love. This love is what we all seek despite the temptations of the sensuous, the erotic, the violent and the perversions of pornography.

"I believe that for the young and the idealistic, my novels with their pure heroines and high ideals are a guide to happiness. Only by seeking the Divine Spark which exists in every human being, can we create a future built on the foundation of faith."

Barbara Cartland is also well known for her Library of Love, classic tales of romance, written by famous authors like Elinor Glyn and Ethel M. Dell, which have been personally selected and specially adapted for today's readers by Miss Cartland.

"These novels I have selected and edited for my 'Library of Love' are all stories with which the readers can identify themselves and also be assured that right will triumph in the end. These tales elevate and activate the mind rather than debase it as so many modern stories do."

Now, in August, Bantam presents the first four novels in a new Barbara Cartland Ancient Wisdom series. The books are THE FORBIDDEN CITY by Barbara Cartland, herself; THE ROMANCE OF TWO WORLDS by Marie Corelli; THE HOUSE OF FULFILLMENT by L. Adams Beck; and BLACK LIGHT by Talbot Mundy.

"Now I am introducing something which I think is of vital importance at this moment in history. Following my own autobiographical book I SEEK THE MIRACULOUS, which Dutton is publishing in hardcover this summer, I am offering those who seek 'the world behind the world' novels which contain, besides a fascinating story, the teaching of Ancient Wisdom.

"In the snow-covered vastnesses of the Himalayas, there are lamaseries filled with manuscripts which have been kept secret for century upon century. In the depths of the tropical jungles and the arid wastes of the deserts, there are also those who know the esoteric mysteries which few can understand.

"Yet some of their precious and sacred knowledge has been revealed to writers in the past. These books I have collected, edited and offer them to those who want to look beyond this greedy, grasping, materialistic world to find their own souls.

"I believe that Love, human and divine, is the jail-breaker of that prison of selfhood which confines and confuses us . . .

"I believe that for those who have attained enlightenment, super-normal (not super-human) powers are available to those who seek them."

*All Barbara Cartland's own novels and her Library of Love are available in Bantam Books, wherever paperbacks are sold. Look for her Ancient Wisdom Series to be available in August.*

# Barbara Cartland

The world's bestselling author of romantic fiction.
Her stories are always captivating tales of intrigue,
adventure and love.

| | | | |
|---|---|---|---|
| ☐ | 2993 | NEVER LAUGH AT LOVE | $1.25 |
| ☐ | 02972 | A DREAM FROM THE NIGHT | $1.25 |
| ☐ | 02987 | CONQUERED BY LOVE | $1.25 |
| ☐ | 10337 | HUNGRY FOR LOVE | $1.25 |
| ☐ | 2917 | DREAM AND THE GLORY | $1.50 |
| ☐ | 10971 | THE RHAPSODY OF LOVE | $1.50 |
| ☐ | 10715 | THE MARQUIS WHO HATED WOMEN | $1.50 |
| ☐ | 10972 | LOOK, LISTEN AND LOVE | $1.50 |
| ☐ | 10975 | A DUEL WITH DESTINY | $1.50 |
| ☐ | 10976 | CURSE OF THE CLAN | $1.50 |
| ☐ | 10977 | PUNISHMENT OF A VIXEN | $1.50 |
| ☐ | 11101 | THE OUTRAGEOUS LADY | $1.50 |
| ☐ | 11168 | A TOUCH OF LOVE | $1.50 |
| ☐ | 11169 | THE DRAGON AND THE PEARL | $1.50 |

**Buy them at your local bookstore or use this handy coupon for ordering:**

# Barbara Cartland

The world's bestselling author of romantic fiction.
Her stories are always captivating tales of intrigue,
adventure and love.

| | | | |
|---|---|---|---|
| ☐ | 11372 | LOVE AND THE LOATHSOME LEOPARD | $1.50 |
| ☐ | 11410 | THE NAKED BATTLE | $1.50 |
| ☐ | 11512 | THE HELL-CAT AND THE KING | $1.50 |
| ☐ | 11537 | NO ESCAPE FROM LOVE | $1.50 |
| ☐ | 11580 | THE CASTLE MADE FOR LOVE | $1.50 |
| ☐ | 11579 | THE SIGN OF LOVE | $1.50 |
| ☐ | 11595 | THE SAINT AND THE SINNER | $1.50 |
| ☐ | 11649 | A FUGITIVE FROM LOVE | $1.50 |
| ☐ | 11797 | THE TWISTS AND TURNS OF LOVE | $1.50 |
| ☐ | 11801 | THE PROBLEMS OF LOVE | $1.50 |
| ☐ | 11751 | LOVE LEAVES AT MIDNIGHT | $1.50 |
| ☐ | 11882 | MAGIC OR MIRAGE | $1.50 |
| ☐ | 10712 | LOVE LOCKED IN | $1.50 |
| ☐ | 11959 | LORD RAVENSCAR'S REVENGE | $1.50 |
| ☐ | 11488 | THE WILD, UNWILLING WIFE | $1.50 |
| ☐ | 11555 | LOVE, LORDS, AND LADY-BIRDS | $1.50 |

# Barbara Cartland's
## Library of Love

**The World's Great Stories of Romance Specially Abridged by Barbara Cartland For Today's Readers.**

| | | | |
|---|---|---|---|
| ☐ | 11487 | **THE SEQUENCE** by Elinor Glyn | $1.50 |
| ☐ | 11468 | **THE BROAD HIGHWAY** by Jeffrey Farnol | $1.50 |
| ☐ | 10927 | **THE WAY OF AN EAGLE** by Ethel M. Dell | $1.50 |
| ☐ | 10926 | **THE REASON WHY** by Elinor Glyn | $1.50 |
| ☐ | 10527 | **THE KNAVE OF DIAMONDS** by Ethel M. Dell | $1.50 |
| ☐ | 11465 | **GREATHEART** by Ethel M. Dell | $1.50 |
| ☐ | 11895 | **HIS OFFICIAL FIANCEE** by Berta Ruck | $1.50 |
| ☐ | 11369 | **THE BARS OF IRON** by Ethel M. Dell | $1.50 |
| ☐ | 11370 | **MAN AND MAID** by Elinor Glyn | $1.50 |
| ☐ | 11391 | **THE SONS OF THE SHEIK** by E. M. Hull | $1.50 |
| ☐ | 12140 | **THE LION TAMER** by E. M. Hull | $1.50 |
| ☐ | 11467 | **THE GREAT MOMENT** by Elinor Glyn | $1.50 |
| ☐ | 12190 | **IT** by Elinor Glyn | $1.50 |
| ☐ | 11816 | **THE PRICE OF THINGS** by Elinor Glyn | $1.50 |
| ☐ | 11821 | **TETHERSTONES** by Ethel M. Dell | $1.50 |